Disney's *Snow White and the Seven Dwarfs* is my all-time favorite fairy-tale movie. Wasn't the music great? I fell in love with the brave, handsome prince. I admired Snow White's beautiful complexion and generous nature. I also admired her housekeeping ability, although I shudder at the thought of cleaning up after seven little men.

Because I'm a writer, I wonder about the story behind the story. When the camera stopped, did those seven men ever drive Snow White straight up the wall? Did they cramp her love life? Did she dream of opening and managing her own mining company? And just how long did that handsome prince have to negotiate with those dwarfs in order to sneak a kiss from Snow White?

The Fairest of Them All didn't start out as Snow White's story. But when my editor called and suggested I add three more dwarfs and a stepmother, I started thinking (after I recovered from shock). The idea was exciting and fun, the possibilities intriguing. This book was a joy to write. I hope it will be a joy for you to read.

Leanne Banks

WHAT ARE *LOVESWEPT* ROMANCES?

They are stories of true romance and touching emotion. We believe those two very important ingredients are constants in our highly sensual and very believable stories in the *LOVESWEPT* line. Our goal is to give you, the reader, stories of consistently high quality that may sometimes make you laugh, sometimes make you cry, but are always fresh and creative and contain many delightful surprises within their pages.

Most romance fans read an enormous number of books. Those they truly love, they keep. Others may be traded with friends and soon forgotten. We hope that each *LOVESWEPT* romance will be a treasure—a "keeper." We will always try to publish

LOVE STORIES YOU'LL NEVER FORGET
BY AUTHORS YOU'LL ALWAYS REMEMBER

The Editors

Loveswept ® 592

Leanne Banks
The Fairest of Them All

BANTAM BOOKS
NEW YORK · TORONTO · LONDON · SYDNEY · AUCKLAND

THE FAIREST OF THEM ALL

A Bantam Book / January 1993

If you would be interested in receiving protective vinyl
covers for your Loveswept books, please write to this address
for information:

Loveswept
Bantam Books
P.O. Box 985
Hicksville, NY 11802

ISBN 0-553-44287-2

Published simultaneously in the United States and Canada

Bantam Books are published by Bantam Books, a division of
Bantam Doubleday Dell Publishing Group, Inc. Its trademark,
consisting of the words "Bantam Books" and the portrayal of
a rooster, is Registered in U.S. Patent and Trademark Office
and in other countries. Marca Registrada. Bantam Books, 666
Fifth Avenue, New York, New York 10103.

PRINTED IN THE UNITED STATES OF AMERICA

OPM   0 9 8 7 6 5 4 3 2 1

To Beth and Nita
who started it all with
"We'd like you to add three more dwarfs. . . ."

Prologue

"I'll never get over him!" wailed seventeen-year-old Carlene Pendleton.

Russ Bradford patted her on the back and looked around. The rented palm would have concealed them if Carly wasn't making such a racket. He'd been taking a breather from his friend Brett's wedding reception when Carly had flopped into his lap and started weeping. Now he was stuck nursing a heartbroken mass of teenage femininity wrapped in layers of chiffon when he'd rather be home watching the baseball game and nursing a beer.

He felt her tears seep through his starched shirt and gave a heavy sigh. "Carly, you gotta get a hold of yourself. You don't want your brothers to see you like this. Think how much teasing you'll have to put up with."

Carly lifted her moist eyes to his and sniffed. "I can't help it. I had such dreams for Brett and me. Now," she choked, "they're all gone."

Russ didn't bother to point out that Carly had

been the one with the dreams, not Brett. In an attempt to divert her, he said, "Hey, in a couple of weeks, you'll start your senior year. You'll probably have guys lined up asking you to the homecoming dance."

The thought gave her pause. She sniffed again. "Think so?"

"Sure," Russ said emphatically. Carly was tall and skinny, and Russ had enough experience with the female gender to know she was definitely a late bloomer. "I bet all the girls wish they had your dark hair and violet eyes. And your brothers are probably gonna have to shoot the male population of Beulah County for whistling at your legs."

"I'm too tall," she said miserably. "The doctor says I'll probably grow at least two more inches. I feel like an ostrich. If I get a date for homecoming, his cheek will be pressed against my rib cage instead of my forehead."

Russ withheld his chuckle. He didn't want to bring on another spate of tears. "I'll tell you what. If you don't get a date for homecoming, I'll come back from the university and take you myself."

"I might as well ask one of my brothers," Carly muttered as she smoothed her frilly dress.

She had a point, Russ thought. He'd grown up with Carly's brothers and had become acquainted with Carly when her biggest problems had been colic and diaper rash.

"Baby, you don't see it now, but everything will come together for you in a year or two. I promise you'll be leaving trails of men in your wake."

"I don't want trails of men," Carly insisted, her eyes filling with tears again. "I w-want B-Brett."

Russ's uneasiness increased tenfold. Carly hardly

ever stuttered anymore. The rare occasion she slipped was a sign of extreme distress.

The balcony door opened, and Russ heard the sound of music and masculine voices. He whipped out a handkerchief and wiped Carly's tears, thinking she was going to kick herself tomorrow if she didn't dry up now.

From longtime experience with the Pendleton clan, he knew there were two things you didn't mess with—pride and independence. "You don't want everybody to get the idea you're a sniveling crybaby, do you?" he asked, aiming directly for her pride.

Carly stiffened. "I am not a sniveling crybaby," she said in a wobbly, but stutter-free voice.

"Then quit acting like one."

Jerking the handkerchief from his hand, she stood, ready to run for the ladies' room. She took two steps, then turned around. She took a deep breath, "Uh, Russ . . ."

"Yeah?"

She gave a shaky version of the smile that made her brothers willing to slay dragons for her. "Thanks."

One

"Hey, babe, you've got a nice swing on that back porch."

Carly Pendleton stopped checking the heavily laden table of hors d'oeuvres and cut her eyes in the direction of that familiar, naughty male voice. She shook her head chidingly. "You're setting a horrible example for these impressionable high school seniors, Russ."

He shrugged his wide shoulders as he played a ballad on the grand piano. "What can I say?" Russ asked innocently. "In six years, you've gotten a rear end that bears watching."

She fought the smile teasing her lips and lost. "I'm surprised you noticed, what with Tina and Amanda." Carly looked heavenward in mock confusion. "Or is Natalie the latest one?"

"You wound me," Russ said. "You know you've always had my heart."

"And I suppose you've donated the rest of your

body to research." Carly arched a dark eyebrow. "Feminine research."

"Well," he said, running his hands up the keyboard in an arpeggio, "if you ever decide you want to conduct a study of your own . . ." He let the thought dangle seductively between them.

Carly's breath caught, then she laughed. After all, Russ wasn't serious. She watched him pick up the wineglass and take a drink. "You know, I never have figured out how you can make your big square hands play such beautiful music on this piano. It just doesn't seem possible." She briefly touched one of his broad fingers.

"Years of practice," he said after she released his hand. "My mother forced me. I took a lot of ribbing until I beat the hell out of a few of my tormentors."

"I never thought of that." Carly smiled. "I owe your mother a debt of gratitude. Who'd have ever thought Beulah County's premier catfish farmer would be playing piano for special occasions on my riverboat?"

"You owe *me* a debt of gratitude," Russ corrected. "I got several black eyes as a result of my music training. The least you could do is console me." He struggled to plaster an unbelievably pitiful expression on his rugged face.

Carly shook her head. Russell Bradford simply could not look pitiful. At thirty, he stood six feet four with over two hundred pounds of weight distributed into well-defined muscle throughout his tanned body. As a child, his hair had been bright red. The years had toned it to a dark auburn. His craggy, mobile face had the ability to both intimidate an opponent and charm the panties off his current conquest. But although he was an outrageous flirt, he kept his practical heart under lock and key.

"My mother always gave my brothers milk and cookies for consolation," she said sweetly. "I can have some sent up from the galley."

"You're breaking my heart, Carly."

"You'll survive." She glanced around the noisy dining room to make sure everyone was having a good time. The graduation party was going off without a hitch, she thought, then turned back to Russ. "By the way, I've had a special request for your services next Thursday night at an anniversary party. Can you make it?"

"You'll have to play me for it," he replied, loading the simple statement with challenge. "Then we'll negotiate."

This was an old routine between them. When she first started the riverboat cruises, she couldn't afford to pay Russ, so they'd played a hand of poker and she'd won. Now, every time she asked him to play the piano, they still played poker and she won every time.

"You're on, Bradford. Get ready to lose. Tomorrow night at the potluck at Aunt Bitsy's okay?"

Russ looked at Carly while she ran a hand through her short, black, attractively mussed hair. Her violet eyes were fringed by spiky dark eyelashes that didn't need mascara. The color in her cheeks came from her emotions, he knew. He'd teased her often enough to cause his share of blushes. She might have bothered to powder her nose that morning, but it was shiny now. She'd probably nibbled the lipstick off her lips five minutes after putting it on. Russ figured he could take care of her lipstick removal in about ten seconds. His mouth buzzed just thinking about it.

He had plans for Carly Pendleton. The way her sultry eyes danced with a daring light made him want to teach her things she'd never learned before. "Tomorrow night's okay. But one of these days," he said roughly, "a man's gonna take you up on your reckless challenges."

The growl in his voice brought an involuntary flutter to her stomach. Carly shook it off. Fighting attraction to Russ was as natural as breathing. In her opinion, a prudent woman brushed her teeth, paid her bills, and took Russ Bradford's provocative masculinity with a grain of salt.

"He'll have to be fast and smart. I'm too busy taking care of business right now." She checked her watch. "We're about to dock, so I'll see you later."

Carly greeted a few guests on her way outside, then stole a moment to enjoy the evening breeze and star-filled night. She felt a rush of affection for her boat and nourished her secret wish of full ownership of *Matilda's Dream*. Sharing it with her seven loving, but overbearing older brothers would try a saint's patience. Somebody up there was giving her a temporary break, though, since three of her brothers were taking a camping trip on the Appalachian Trail.

Carly knew full ownership was more of an emotional issue than a financial one. Her childhood had left her with an aching private need for something or someone to call her own. Someones tended to be unreliable, so Carly had chosen *Matilda's Dream*.

Watching the boat dock, Carly thought of her distant, unreachable father and her remote stepmother. Even now, the pain cut deep. Some dreams, she'd learned, never come true.

• • •

As Carly finished setting the redwood table in the backyard for dinner, she looked up at the threatening clouds and worried. She had a full boat tonight. If it rained, the galley crew would be pulling extra duty.

Russ strolled up beside her. "What are you scowling at?"

"If it rains, it'll flood the galley." She twisted her hands. "They've got a full boat. I should be there."

"Are you telling me your crew doesn't know what to do with buckets and mops?"

"Well, no." A reluctant smile tugged at her mouth. When he put it in such a matter-of-fact way, her anxiety seemed ridiculous.

"Then don't worry." He took her elbow and ushered her toward the dessert table set up under a weeping willow. "Enjoy your family. Enjoy the food. Enjoy me."

Carly stumbled and felt a flush steal across her face. "I think I'll start with the brownies," she said dryly and scooped up one from the table. "Three more groups have asked you to play the piano at their parties within the next two months. Do you think you can do it?"

"I'll play poker for it." Russ stole a large crumb of her brownie and put it in his mouth. Then he licked his lips.

Watching the agile motion of his slick tongue, Carly felt a tug of curiosity. His mouth was wet and clever. And Russ was probably equally clever in the ways of using his mouth to steal the breath and sanity from a woman. For an instant, she wanted to know how it would feel to have his undivided sensual attention.

Feeling his gaze on her, she looked into his caramel eyes. He stared at her for a long moment.

Her throat grew tight. Could he possibly know what she was thinking? How humiliating, she thought. Forcing her mind back to business, she cleared her throat. "Let me get some cards. Is the living room okay? The kitchen's busy right now."

"The living room's fine." He rested his hand on her shoulder and rubbed the nape of her neck with a callused thumb. "Lead on."

He walked close enough for her to feel the heat from his body, and that small movement of his thumb had her breath coming too quickly. Russ didn't usually touch her this much, or maybe she'd never noticed before.

"Watch that croquet bracket," Russ said in a low voice that rumbled along her nerve endings. He wrapped a steadying hand around her rib cage, brushing the underside of her breast. Carly nearly fell flat on her face. A gasp locked in her throat. A couple of inches higher, she thought, and he'd be palming her breast, rubbing her nipple.

Carly clenched her jaw, fighting his effect on her. She'd always been able to shake off her awareness of Russ. Why couldn't she now?

By the time she sat across from Russ in the living room, she felt rattled. She thrust the cards at him. "You deal."

He nodded. "Same as usual. Whiskey poker. One hand." He shuffled and dealt the cards one at a time to her, to the "widow" in the middle, and then to him.

Carly noticed his hands, the broad square fingers

and rough calluses. With his shirtsleeves rolled up, her attention was drawn to his forearms, brown and muscled, dusted with light sun-bleached hair. She'd felt those arms around her and never realized how . . .

"Carly," Russ prompted. "Don't you want to pick up your cards?"

Carly blinked, then quickly gathered the cards from the table. The hand wasn't great, but she'd beat him with worse. He was terrible at poker. Carly always won. She kept the two fours and traded the other three cards.

She tried not to grimace at what she got.

Russ traded two of his cards and thoughtfully rubbed his chin.

She traded two cards. The result brought her another four. Not bad, but she didn't trust him. He wasn't joking or talking as he usually did when they played.

It was Russ's turn, and he knocked on the cherry table.

Carly raised her eyebrows. Knocking meant she had one more chance to trade before they showed their hands. After trading, she drew one more four. A rush of adrenaline shot through her. She would beat him again.

"I hope you're keeping brushed up on anniversary songs," Carly said confidently and laid down her cards with a flourish. "Four of a kind."

The barest hint of a smile played around Russ's eyes. He didn't look at his cards as he turned them over. He watched Carly's face instead.

Carly gasped in shock as she stared at his winning hand. "A straight flush! How did you do that? You've never had a straight flush before." She looked at his face. "You won!" she said in an accusing voice.

Russ laughed. "I guess I finally got lucky. It's about time, isn't it?"

She was still shaking her head over the outcome when the consequence came to mind. "I guess I'll have to pay you now."

His smile fell. She noticed his jaw tighten before he picked up the cards and shuffled them. "I've never taken money for playing the piano. It wouldn't feel right. But I'd be willing to negotiate."

Negotiate. That word again. Carly grew suspicious. She opened her mouth to refuse until she remembered her goals for the summer. She needed Russ for these parties. He was part of the draw. The people probably wanted him as much as they wanted *Matilda's Dream.*

It wasn't that his piano playing was so superb. It was more the easy and relaxed mood he set for a party. He talked with the guests and took requests, occasionally led everyone in a sing-along.

She sighed. "Okay. What do you want? A private moonlight cruise with your latest favorite lady?" The idea pinched her insides but she said it anyway. "Do you want me to go over your books for free? Or," she finished tongue in cheek, "do you need some help harvesting those ugly fish of yours?"

"None of the above." He rose from the armchair and made his way over to her. "I've got a problem," he said thoughtfully. "And I think you can help me with it."

"Problem?" He sounded serious. Concern washed over her as she stared at him. He didn't appear ill. "You're not sick, are you?"

He wiped a broad hand across his mouth to hide a

smile and sat beside her. "Not sick. More like harassed. You know how the Ladies Auxiliary at church—" He broke off, spying the Band-Aid on her thigh.

He circled the bandage with his index finger. Her skin was velvety soft. Her feminine scent wove around him, and he completely forgot her overprotective brothers were within shouting distance. The hem of her white shorts lay about an inch from his finger. Russ was so aware of just how close his hand was to her feminine secrets that his hand shook.

He brought his finger to his mouth and kissed it, then returned it to the bandage on her thigh. When her leg trembled beneath his touch, his dark gaze shot up to hers.

Carly struggled for breath. The innocent notion of kissing it to make it better took on a totally different meaning. Russ was so big, so male, sitting there in an ordinary cotton shirt and faded jeans that suddenly seemed to scream his virility.

There wasn't anything different about him, she told herself. He'd always been both gentle and playful with her. He'd always sat that way, feet planted firmly on the ground, legs spread wide. Her gaze fell to the area that gloved his masculinity, and a staggering excitement raced through her.

Appalled at the direction of her thoughts, Carly jerked her leg away from his touch. She felt like a complete idiot. Inhaling sharply, she admonished herself to speak slowly.

"I was climbing over one of the fences, and I got scratched." Was that pitiful, wobbly voice hers? Giving herself a hard mental shake, she continued more forcefully. "You were saying something about a problem."

Russ cleared his throat and leaned back. "The Ladies Auxiliary has me targeted for this summer. You know how they find an eligible bachelor and shove every available female under his nose until he either marries one of them or moves away."

Carly nodded, remembering how her oldest brother Daniel had actually left town for an entire summer. The older ladies of Beulah County took seriously their duty of making matches for the younger population.

"I just don't have time for it this year," Russ explained. "And there are several community activities I'm expected to attend."

Carly frowned, wondering how he wanted her to assist him. "Russ, I wish I could help, but I don't see how. I have no influence on those ladies. It's not like I attend their meetings or anything."

"Well, I wasn't asking you to speak on my behalf." He leaned forward. "I want you to be my escort for the summer. That would keep them off my back," he told her in his most unromantic voice.

"Your escort?" Carly stood, trying to comprehend him. "For the entire summer! Then everyone would think we're involved." That was only her first objection.

Russ shrugged. "Yeah."

She narrowed her eyes. "This could mess up your, uh, other romantic liaisons."

He gave her a direct gaze. "I don't have any other romantic liaisons. Besides, it's a small price to pay. The Ladies Auxiliary is relentless."

She rubbed her pounding forehead. Something about this just didn't seem right. "Why didn't you ask someone else? Someone who appeals to you."

"Because," he said patiently as he stood, "someone else would misunderstand my intentions. You won't."

That sensible explanation should have reassured her, but it didn't. Her confusion suddenly cleared and in its place came anger. "What you want," she began in a slow, quiet voice, "is for me to pretend I'm your"—she groped for an adequate term—"your adoring romantic interest for the summer. I would be at your disposal to attend activities, during which time the gossips would have a field day over our affair."

Russ's jaw tightened.

Carly ignored it. "Come September, we would stop seeing each other, and I'd have to deal with pity from every Tom, Dick, and Harry on the street. Have you—"

"That's not necessarily true," Russ interjected. "They might think you dumped me."

"Oh sure," she said with complete disbelief. "Exactly how many women have dumped you, Russ?"

Russ put his hands on his hips and sighed. "There was probably someone in high school. Hell, I don't know, Carly. All I know is you need a piano player and I need a female escort. We've always been pals, so there'd be no harm in it."

He shrugged his powerful shoulders once again. "As far as your reputation is concerned, everybody knows your brothers practically keep you under lock and key and that you're as innocent now as the day you were born. Seeing me won't change that."

With each placating word, she became more insulted. She'd never been particularly confident of her feminine allure. To know that Russ viewed her as a nonwoman hurt. There was no basis for her feelings and that only made her more upset.

She had only one thing to say to him.

"G-G-Go t-to hell!"

For one endless second, she watched shock envelop his face. Then, completely mortified, she turned on her heel and left the room. She instinctively raced for the back door. So caught up in her humiliation, she barely noticed the astonished faces of her brothers in the hall.

Aunt Bitsy asked her to take a bowl of ice outside. Carly complied, but her final instruction to Russ rang through her mind like a chord played on a poorly tuned piano.

She winced. It had been six years since she'd stuttered.

Back in the parlor, Russ was trying to collect his thoughts when Carly's brothers entered. He had a couple of seconds' grace before they started in on him in descending order.

"What was that all about, Russ?" Daniel began.

"You've been playing poker again," Garth said, pointing at the cards on the cherry table.

Jarod's mouth was tight with disapproval. "Carly's never told anybody to go to hell before."

Then finally Troy offered the most telling piece of information. "She stuttered," he said accusingly.

Four pairs of violet eyes stared at him, waiting for an explanation. If Ethan, Nathan, and Brick were here, they'd be staring him down too. Another man might have trembled in his boots, but Russ had known the Pendletons a long time. He'd played football with two of them, shared a college dorm room with Garth, and worked alongside all of them after a vicious tornado tore through their daddy's farm.

They were the closest thing to brothers he had. They could also be a pain in the ass.

"We played whiskey poker, and she lost," Russ said simply.

Garth's mouth twisted ruefully. A chuckle escaped from him, then another. Soon, the room was filled with masculine laughter.

"Carly always did hate to lose," Daniel said.

"She was madder than a hornet. You probably should have let her win, Russ," Troy pointed out.

Russ shook his head. "No. Carly's tired of being treated like a child. She's ready to stand on her own two feet."

"Yeah, but she's a girl," Troy said.

"Do you remember how you felt when people kept calling you a boy after you turned twenty?" Russ asked. "Do you remember what you did to prove you weren't a boy?"

They all remembered. Russ could read it on their faces. He remembered the struggle for manhood himself, the taking of a woman not out of love, not even out of respect, but out of an empty search for proof.

The atmosphere in the room grew thoughtful.

Daniel cleared his throat. "You're trying to tell us something."

"Nothing you don't already know," Russ said gently. "Carly's a woman. She still needs you, but not in the same way she used to."

Troy shifted his stance. "But if we don't look after her, who will?"

Russ wanted to say that he would, that they needn't worry. But that wouldn't solve the problem. She didn't want to be taken care of. "I think Carly wants to look after herself. If she doesn't get some space, she might decide she needs to prove herself. And you don't want that."

They all muttered their agreement.

The men grew uncomfortable with the serious discussion and found excuses to leave the room. Garth, however, hung back and when the others had left, he turned to Russ.

"You want her," he said bluntly.

Russ's lip curved grimly. "You know me well."

Garth shook his tousled dark head and sighed. "I don't know if she's ready for this, Russ."

"I'm not waiting any longer. I've been planning this for two years."

Garth's eyes widened in surprise. "Two years? I guess this isn't just one of your flings, then."

Russ understood the question. After all, when they had roomed together in college, Garth had seen the number and variety of females that had paraded in and out of his life. "I mean business," Russ assured him. "Cut me some slack. Between you and your brothers and Carly's drive for independence, this summer is going to be pure hell."

Garth chuckled and gave Russ a commiserating pat on the shoulder. Russ shoved his hands into his pockets and sighed. He was determined to remain clearheaded and objective. With painful accuracy, he recalled the one time he'd acted impulsively and the disastrous results. He'd made a complete fool of himself during his brief ill-fated marriage, and *it wouldn't happen again.* Russ prided himself on his ability to extricate himself from emotionally volatile situations. As a matter of fact, he'd given Carly's brothers a tip or two on the subject.

Shaking his head, Russ thought back to Carly's parting comment. He hadn't counted on the full scope of her feminine pride. He'd tried to make his request as nonthreatening as possible. In trying to reassure her, he'd obviously botched his plan. Now he had to figure out how to get things back on track.

The next morning, Carly was late for church. She scooted in the last wooden pew, not wanting to draw attention to her tardiness. It was those crazy erotic dreams. She'd tossed and turned a good part of the night, then overslept this morning. And it was all Russ Bradford's fault.

The ushers took the offering, and the choir sang a soothing hymn. The quiet setting had just begun to calm her when Russ appeared beside her pew. Carly tensed, but moved over.

She kept her gaze fixed straight ahead at the pastor, although she couldn't hear a word he said.

Russ leaned over and murmured in her ear, "To err is human."

She remained silent.

"Are you ever going to speak to me again?" he whispered.

Giving up her pretense of paying attention, Carly sighed. "I haven't decided. I'm torn between wringing your neck and apologizing for telling you to go to—" She broke off, remembering she was in church. Even though God knew what she'd said to Russ, she didn't think she needed to refresh His memory.

"Let me take you to lunch," Russ murmured.

She cut her eyes at him and started to shake her head.

"No strings," he whispered.

The older woman in front of them turned around and frowned. Carly pointed at Russ. The woman's frown turned to a smile. Carly looked at the ceiling.

"Lunch," he murmured again.

"Be quiet," Carly said.

"Lunch."

Carly was caught in a dilemma. She wanted her easy friendship with Russ back, but she had to get rid of this new awareness first. It was making her do crazy things, think crazy thoughts.

"It's not like I'm asking you to go to bed," Russ whispered.

Her heart jumped. Shocked, Carly's head whipped around. He couldn't possibly know she'd dreamed that very scenario this morning.

She studied him carefully. His brown eyes held the same lazy humor as always. His body appeared relaxed, with one ankle propped across the opposite knee, and one arm resting behind her on the top of the pew. If she were just a little closer, his big hand might be on her shoulder or back. Her stomach fluttered.

Something about the set of his mouth told her he wasn't going to give up.

"Will you be quiet?" she asked in her softest voice.

"Lunch."

"Yes," she whispered tersely.

Two

Carly was relieved Russ didn't begin a discussion about the pastor's sermon. Since she'd spent the rest of the service mentally rehearsing all the logical reasons why she couldn't be his summer escort, she could only guess what the pastor had talked about.

Russ had suggested the Davy Crockett Diner. She politely agreed. He ordered steak. She ordered chicken.

She expected him to begin negotiations any minute.

Russ loosened his burgundy-print tie. "I met your new assistant last night. She told me you're looking for new entertainment."

Carly nodded and relaxed. "For the cruises with meals. I think it would draw more customers, but I don't want to spend a lot of money."

He smiled at the waitress as she served their iced tea and tossed salads.

"Have you thought about a disc jockey?"

"Yes, but they're so loud." Carly took a sip of her

drink. "I don't know what I want. Just something different."

"Why don't you let your waitstaff pull double duty? Maybe they could serve drinks and dessert, then do some kind of musical comedy act."

Carly considered the idea and felt a spark of excitement. "That's wonderful. I could hire some community college students. Their schedules would be flexible." She beamed at him. "Thanks."

"You're welcome."

Carly took a bite of her salad and made a mental note to contact the community college tomorrow. After a moment, she noticed that Russ was still looking at her. She felt a curious tugging in her stomach.

"So you think the idea will help?"

"Yes, thanks for sharing it with me." She had a niggling feeling he expected something besides thanks from her. Then the light dawned.

"Exactly how much is this idea going to cost me, Russ?"

Russ raised his hands. "Hey, I'm on your side. Consider it a token of my friendship."

Carly nodded and went back to her salad.

"Of course, if you found it in your heart to return the favor . . ."

Glancing back up at him, she noted the guileless expression on his face. His eyes, however, were pure temptation. She gave up on her salad. "I don't suppose you have any ideas about how I could return the favor?"

"Well," he said, slowly rubbing his chin, "since you brought it up, there is one thing."

"Uh-huh," Carly said.

He bobbed an ice cube with one of his fingers.

"What I need is a beautiful, intelligent woman who will let me take her out to dinner and community functions for the next few months."

He glanced back at her. "I find I have a preference for a tall, leggy riverboat owner with short, dark hair and violet eyes. And a smile a man would kill for."

His warm gaze fell on her eyes, then her mouth. Despite reason, Carly's heart fluttered. Her cheeks heated. She felt charmed and flattered. She almost believed the snake. It was on the tip of her tongue to accept. What woman would turn away this delicious, undivided attention from such a sexy man?

Then she came to her senses. "Have you considered the personal ads?"

A reluctant grin tugged at his mouth as he shook his head. "Carly, this is no way to treat a buddy."

That was the problem. She didn't see Russ as just a buddy. She saw him as a desirable man. Although his teasing was intended as innocent fun, she could easily envision herself getting hurt under the constant onslaught of his brand of masculine attention. Everybody knew Russ Bradford changed women as often as a college freshman changed majors.

She risked an assessing glance at him. Since his brief disastrous marriage, no woman had ever touched Russ's heart. When things got sticky, Russ extricated himself from the situation. He had the ability to hold his emotions aloof. After her childhood, Carly needed a man who wore his heart on his sleeve.

Just then, the waitress set their steaming entrées on the table, and Russ led the conversation in other, less volatile directions.

They talked about her new brochure. She asked about his mother who had moved to Florida after Russ's father's death.

One of Carly's clients, Francine Granger, and her husband stopped by their table. "Carly, you're just the person I've been wanting to talk to. We need to confirm my reservation for our anniversary party on your riverboat." Francine gave her balding husband an affectionate squeeze. "Norman and I have been married for twenty-five years, and we want a big celebration."

Carly smiled at the effervescent Francine and long-suffering Norman. She'd bet money that Norman would be happy with a quiet dinner at home, but she wouldn't quibble. Francine's anniversary party promised to be as extravagant as the woman herself.

"Russ, you will be able to play the piano for us, won't you?" Francine continued.

Carly's stomach sank. She and Russ still hadn't resolved the issue, and she didn't want to lose Francine's business.

The middle-aged woman, who happened to be a member of the Ladies Auxiliary, fixed an appraising eye on Russ. "You know, Russ, my daughter Caroline will be visiting from graduate school soon. She'll need someone to take her around. Do you think you could—"

Russ cleared his throat and threw a meaningful glance at Carly. "As far as my playing for your party, that's totally up to Carly."

She could have killed him. He'd boxed her in. Francine and Norman were waiting for her reply. If she refused, she might lose the business. If she accepted, she'd be obligated to Russ for the entire summer.

Slowly, as if the words were squeezed from her, Carly said, "Russ will play for your party." Then her mind snatched another idea. The corners of her mouth turned up into a bright smile. "As for Caroline, Russ is—"

"Completely booked," Russ interjected smoothly. He shot her a grin that somehow mixed triumph and sensual promise. "I've got all sorts of plans for this summer."

The Grangers murmured good-bye while Carly glared at Russ. "That was dirty," she hissed after they left.

Russ shook his head. "That's negotiation. I give you something you want." His warm gaze lingered on her lips. "You give me something I want."

Her heart jumped into her throat. Carly knew his explanation was pragmatic, but that didn't explain her dizziness. She cleared her throat. "And what do you want?"

"I'm attending a banquet next Saturday where I'm supposed to present an award. I need you to go with me." He shrugged. "Natalie's been hinting about rings I won't be buying her."

Carly felt a stab of disappointment. Ever practical, Russ sensed when a woman was getting too close and preferred to take care of it in an expedient way. She sighed in defeat. Grudgingly, she asked, "What time?"

"Five-thirty," he said as they stood to leave. "And heels would be nice, Carly." Russ ignored her startled expression. He'd thrown in that last request as a test. She hated wearing heels. Opening the door, Russ stifled the urge to let out a victory yell. His plan was working.

It hit Carly late one night when she was going through some correspondence at the office. She shoved aside the bills and thank-you notes from the local police and senior citizens group.

Carly almost tossed the form letter announcing the opening of Central Tennessee's Women and Children's Center. One of the support groups, however, struck her as if she were an unarmed soldier.

Children who have lost a parent.

She should be past it, but her memories were ruthlessly vivid. She remembered a five-year-old girl struggling with the death of her mother, crying alone in bed. How many nights had she called for Mommy or Daddy and neither had come?

She rubbed her cheeks, surprised to find them damp. She remembered the stuttering. She remembered reaching out to her daddy only to have him turn away. It had gotten worse when her stepmother Eunice entered the scene. Looking back, Carly realized she'd lost both parents at the same time. While her stuttering had inspired her brothers' protective nature to epic proportions, her father had become more distant.

Carly had spent the first part of her life trying to reach an unreachable man. A man who kept his emotions to himself. She wouldn't do it again. She'd tried hard to please her stepmother when her stepmother didn't want to be pleased.

An uneasiness settled deep in her stomach at the thought. Although Russ was kind, he scrupulously avoided emotional involvement. Could she spend the summer pretending to be his romantic interest and remain unaffected?

Carly thought of Russ's sexy mouth and shuddered. *You're dead meat.*

Disgusted with her weakness, she thumped her desk. She would just have to remind herself that

Russ would never be serious about her. Russ liked to play. When things got emotional, he tended to leave. She needed a man who could handle the tender side of a relationship.

With that plan in mind, Carly felt comforted. She looked at the letter again. She couldn't volunteer. It would hurt too much. She could, however, offer a cruise as a special outing for the children. Going with her instincts, she wrote a letter to the center and sent it off.

At twenty-nine minutes after five on Saturday night, Carly was tearing through the bottom of her closet in search of heels. She pulled out a pair of pink fuzzy bedroom slippers, tennis shoes, and black patent leather flats. She felt hopeful when she found a white sandal with a real heel, but she couldn't find its mate.

The doorbell rang, and she cursed. "Just a minute," she called. What was wrong with her? This was just Russ, for Pete's sake. She took a deep breath and stood. Smoothing the little black knit dress over her hips, she attempted to regain her composure.

She glanced into the mirror and approved the contrast between her freshwater pearl choker and the black jewel neckline. After ruffling her hair and applying red lipstick, Carly scooted into the black patent flats and went to open the door.

Russ stood there, bigger than she remembered, rendering her temporarily shy. He wore a brown nubby silk sport coat that accented his broad shoulders. His dark red hair was brushed back, but part of it fell attractively over his forehead. Sexy, she thought. Then she clamped her teeth into her lip before it could quiver.

As the silence continued, a grin played around the edges of his brown eyes, but not his mouth. Carly felt like a gawky adolescent again, and she didn't like it one bit.

Russ gave her just enough time to become uneasy, then said, "You look good." He touched one of her dangling earrings. "Pretty. Are you ready?"

Carly breathed carefully. "Yeah." Then she laughed at herself and closed the door behind her. "I never asked you who's sponsoring this banquet."

"The chamber of commerce. You might be able to drum up some business while we're there." He glanced pointedly at her feet. "No heels?"

"High heels hurt my feet. You're such a practical man I'm surprised you like them."

He looked her over once again. "Every man has his weaknesses. Why don't we skip the banquet and go back inside? I'll tell you all about mine."

An instant surge of heat sped through her veins. He wasn't serious, she reminded herself. But the image of Russ, naked and aroused, giving and demanding, robbed her of speech. She cleared her throat. "You need to present an award," she reminded him, walking toward his car. "And I'm hungry."

"So am I," Russ said in a sexy growl behind her.

Carly spent the short drive telling herself not to wonder what kind of hunger Russ was talking about and exactly what breathtaking methods he would use to appease that hunger. By the time they arrived, she was gritting her teeth with the effort.

She and Russ entered the hotel banquet room where rows of tables dressed in white tablecloths and candlelight created an elegant mood. They were seated across from Natalie Conner and her date, Bob Miller, the new electronics company representative.

A voluptuous blonde with sexy, reproachful brown eyes, Natalie had been the darling of Beulah County High School when Carly had been an awkward nobody. Natalie was the kind of woman who somehow always seemed to make Carly feel less confident. It wasn't just Natalie's appearance. It was her manner. Even now, Carly had to resist the feelings of inadequacy the other woman's presence generated.

"Russ, honey, when will you be taking your catfish to the processor again?" Natalie asked with an adoring smile.

"In another two months," Russ answered simply.

Carly took another sip of her wine, swirled it around in her mouth, and wondered if it would taste better as the evening wore on.

Russ went to the podium to present the award for best new business contribution to the community, and Natalie finally acknowledged Carly. "That's a cute little dress you have on, Carly. I wouldn't have thought someone with your height could wear that style."

While Carly tried to decide if that was a compliment or not, Russ returned to the table. Dancing began, and Natalie immediately pulled him onto the floor.

A furrow of irritation crossed Russ's face, and Carly felt unexplainably consoled. She noticed his warm gaze returning to her throughout the dance. It made her feel attractive, desirable. . . . Carly rolled her eyes. What she really felt was crazy.

"Would you like to dance?" Bob asked.

"Why not?" Carly said with forced enthusiasm.

They shuffled along to the lovelorn song the band played. "She's kind of overwhelming, isn't she?" Bob asked.

"Natalie?"

"Yeah. She works for my boss. I didn't understand why she gave me the big rush about coming to this banquet at first. Now I do." Bob pushed his tortoiseshell glasses up on his thin nose.

Carly attempted to think of something kind to say about Natalie Conner. Glancing over at Natalie and Russ, she saw the woman press her well-endowed body into him and run her red fingernails through his hair. Carly gave up on saying something nice and switched the subject. "Have you been with National Electronics long?"

"Several years."

She'd just suggested National Electronics hold their next company social on *Matilda's Dream* when Russ cut in.

"You're not holding up your end of the bargain," Russ said in a no-nonsense voice as he took her into his arms.

Carly blinked. "What are you talking about?"

"You're supposed to act like you're happy to be with me instead of hustling Natalie's date."

"Well, Bob's been a little more accessible. The way Natalie plastered herself against you, I'd have needed dynamite to blow you two apart."

Carly felt his shoulder muscles tense beneath her hand, but she continued anyway. "Besides, you didn't say anything about me fawning over you when I agreed to come to this banquet."

Russ's voice became very quiet. "If I wanted fawning, I could have Natalie." His arms tightened, drawing her even closer. "I know it'll be tough, but for the next few minutes, pretend you find me attractive."

Her breath hitched in her throat. She wouldn't have to pretend, she realized. Intellectually, she'd always known that Russ's body was hard and firmly muscled, but she'd never noticed it as a woman would. In her present position, with her breasts heavy against his chest, her stomach fluttering against his abdomen, and his powerful thighs twined with hers, she was fully, femininely aware of him.

"Attractive," she repeated in an unsteady voice.

Russ raised her hand to his cheek and nuzzled it. "Pretend you feel possessive about me." When he lowered his mouth to the vulnerable skin just below her ear and made that same nuzzling motion, her heart jumped into her throat.

"Pretend we're lovers," he whispered into her ear.

His words hit her with such force, she would swear both the walls and the floor of the banquet room rocked and trembled. Her knees felt like Jello-O, and her head was cloudier than the sky during an electric storm.

For one brief moment, Carly stared into Russ's eyes and saw the eyes of a hunter, hungry and predatory. She looked at his mouth and felt an achy emptiness inside her.

Then someone jostled her, and she came to her senses. Heat scored her cheeks. *This was Russ.*

"Have you lost your mind?" she asked breathlessly. "If you wanted Natalie to back off, you should have picked someone more believable. She's never been threatened by me."

"She is now," he said mildly.

"Oh, yeah?" Carly couldn't keep the disbelief from her voice. "Why?"

"You've got me."

Carly opened her mouth to retort, but to her consternation, no clever words came to mind. She frowned.

The music stopped, and Russ caught her off guard, bringing her hand to his warm mouth. He kissed her bandaged finger. "What'd you do this time?"

A quiver danced through her. She slowly released the breath he'd stopped. "Boo-boo of the week," Carly said and took another breath. Where had all the oxygen gone? "I had an argument with a paring knife, and it won." She smiled and removed her hand from his, eager to put some space between them.

Russ guided her back to the table. "I think we can leave now," he murmured, allowing his lips to brush her ear. "Unless you want to stay?"

Carly resisted the urge to rub away the effect of that distracting caress. Instead, she shook her head.

After a perfunctory good-bye to Natalie and Bob, Russ nudged her toward the exit. When they reached the car, she slumped into the leather seat with a sigh. "Well, tonight won't have been a total loss if National Electronics starts giving me some of their business."

Russ revved the powerful engine and backed out of the parking space. "I'm sure Bob will be calling you," he said none too happily, recalling the interested expression on the other man's face.

"Good. I'll be that much closer to my goal," Carly mumbled and closed her eyes.

Russ's ears pricked up. "What goal?"

Carly sighed again. "I want to buy out my—" She broke off abruptly and sat up straighter.

"Buy out my what?" He looked at her. She was almost squirming in her seat. "Is it a secret?"

A long silence followed. "I guess it is."

He didn't push. From past experience, Russ knew that pushing her was a mistake. "If it's important to you, then I hope it works out."

Out of the corner of his eye, he saw her relax slightly.

"It is important. Maybe even vital. And I'll make it happen or die trying."

Russ steered the car into a vacant parking space in her small apartment complex. He placed a hand on her delicate shoulder, loving the feel of her warmth and softness. "Well, I wouldn't want you to kill yourself," he said with a lazy grin. "But let me know if I can help you out."

She wavered. It was only a few seconds, but he saw it in her eyes before she straightened and set her chin.

"I've got to do this myself." She softened the statement with a smile. "But thanks anyway."

Russ resisted the urge to pull her into his lap and kiss the resistance out of her. He trailed his fingers down her arm. "Time for all hardworking ladies to get to bed. Will you share yours with me? I've got a long drive back to the farm."

He heard her soft gasp. Then she hooted with laughter.

"Give me a break, Bradford. When it comes to meaningless flirtations, you wrote the book—and sold it to my brothers. A woman would have to be crazy to take you seriously." Carly smiled and poked his chest. "If you've got such a long drive, you'd better get moving." Then she opened the car door and got out.

Russ watched her long legs and sweet rear end as she edged out. He felt the familiar heat, rubbed his mouth, and wondered if a man could die from being too patient.

He narrowed his eyes. His past was coming back to haunt him. He hadn't counted on Carly not taking him seriously. This wasn't part of his careful plan.

Now, if he rushed his seduction of her, Carly would think he was treating her like any other woman he'd dated. Which was the furthest thing from the truth. So what he must do, he realized grimly, was take it slow.

Giving a long-suffering groan, he followed her to her door. He watched her turn around to face him. Her hair was soft and feathery looking. The light played on her skin, making it look like satin. His hands itched to touch her so badly, he stuck them in his pockets.

"I'll see you Thursday for the Hendersons' anniversary."

Russ nodded, studying her carefully. She cleared her throat and backed in the direction of the door. Was she nervous? His chest swelled with pride. He looked at her mouth and thought again about kissing her. Much as he wanted to, the time wasn't right. He didn't want to scare her off. When he leaned forward, he saw her eyes flutter in a feminine show of nerves, and he smiled inside. Then he kissed her on the forehead, just as one of her brothers would.

"Good night, Carly," he murmured in a low voice and turned to leave.

He was almost all the way down the steps before he heard her soft reply. "Good night, Russ."

It had taken her that long to form a response. Russ smiled on the outside that time.

But he shook his head when he recalled her flat shoes. He had a long way to go.

Three

Could a person die of sexual curiosity? Carly wondered three weeks later as she brooded over a mailorder fashion catalog. Thus far, she'd escorted Russ to two functions, both business related. Since he was the most successful aquaculture farmer in the state, he was often asked to give speeches to assorted organizations. Plus, as an officer of Catfish Farmers of America, it was his duty to promote the eating of catfish at every opportunity.

They'd attended a fish fry put on by a volunteer fire department in a neighboring county. Then they'd driven into Chattanooga for a state tourism meeting. The second meeting had been especially beneficial for Carly as she had used the opportunity to promote *Matilda's Dream*.

On both occasions, Russ had been attentive and charming. Just when she started to relax, he would whisper something naughty and teasing in her ear, or put his arm around her waist, or finger her earrings, or stare at her mouth in the most disconcerting way.

In spite of her resolve, Carly studied that firm, naughty mouth of his and spent a great deal of time anticipating how it would feel pressed against hers. She wondered how his bare chest would feel against her breasts.

At the end of both evenings, however, Russ kissed her forehead and disappeared down the steps, leaving Carly feeling disappointed and restless.

Carly scowled. Russ was totally wrong for her even if he sent her hormones into overdrive. She should be relieved she wasn't forced to fight him off.

Instead, she began to worry about her image.

She knew she'd been terribly overprotected by her brothers. Of course, she'd dated a few men, always under the watchful eye of her brothers. To be perfectly honest, though, none of her suitors had tempted her enough to trade her chastity belt for a wild night in bed.

Presently, Carly was finding both the chastity belt and her pure reputation a strain. Being with Russ made her want to . . . experiment. Did Russ ever think of her as a desirable woman? Did he *ever* want to kiss her?

She discussed it in a roundabout way with her assistant Sara one afternoon. "Have you ever thought about getting your ears pierced?"

Sara pushed aside her long brown hair to reveal tiny gold studs. "My ears are pierced. See?"

"No," Carly shook her head. "I mean several times."

"Why?"

"I don't know." Carly sighed and looked at her daily planner without seeing it. "Maybe to change your image."

Sara sniffed. "I don't allow enough time in my

schedule to put in three pairs of earrings every day. Do you?"

Carly thought about that and shook her head. "No." She started to go back into her inner office, then turned back around, tilting her head thoughtfully. "What about high heels?"

"I like my feet." Sara glanced down at her plain flats. "Why should I torture them?"

"Yeah," Carly agreed, feeling foolish.

"This isn't really about earrings or heels, is it?"

Carly hesitated. With the exception of her oldest brother, her entire family had warmed to her solemn, understated assistant. And since Sara had revealed that her parents were dead and she wished she had some relatives, Carly felt reluctant to say anything negative about her brothers.

"I'm just rethinking my image," she finally said.

Sara nodded. "Have your brothers been making you crazy?"

"No," Carly said, then smiled ironically. "At least not lately. With Ethan, Nathan, and Brick on that camping trip, things have been pretty quiet. But there have been some comments different people have made that have bothered me."

"Like?"

Her smile fell. "Like Carly's always been so shy and reserved. Like you're just not that kind of girl." Her voice became more clipped. "Like everybody knows you're as innocent as the day you were born."

"Hmm," Sara said.

"Hmm what?"

Sara smiled slowly. "Sounds like you'd like to be tarnished."

Carly thought about all the ways she could be

tarnished. Most of those ways involved Russ Bradford. She sighed. "Yeah."

"Well, I've never set out to be tarnished. But if I
wanted to . . . be tarnished, I think I'd wear something from one of these catalogs."

To Carly's surprise, sensible Sara pulled out a
half-dozen mail-order catalogs with clothes that accented the physical attributes of a woman.

Carly took them all home that night and called in
an order before she lost her nerve.

Russ drove to Carly's apartment and prepared
himself for another easygoing, nonthreatening date.
He didn't really want to go to the mayor's dinner
party. What he wanted was to get some burning
questions answered. Like, what did Carly wear to
bed and how long would it take to get it off her? What
color were her nipples and what did they taste like?
Would she sigh or gasp when he spread her thighs
and moved between them?

Russ groaned. His carefully planned strategy was
starting to wear on his nerves, he thought darkly. It
was pure hell keeping his hands off Carly every time
he gave her that brotherly good-night peck at the
door.

Still he didn't want to scare her off. He needed to
lure her slowly, but so completely that she wouldn't
question it when he suggested they make love. That
was the plan. Just the thought of having Carly in his
arms and in his bed made his palms sweat.

Russ knocked and waited patiently at her apartment door until she peeked out. She smiled a little
uncertainly, but her eyes sparkled with excitement.

He wondered at the curious combination of emotions until she opened the door the rest of the way.

She wore the most unvirginal white dress he'd ever seen in his life. It fell off one tanned shoulder, then molded to her curves with breath-stealing clarity. It showed more leg than it concealed. By the time Russ snapped his jaw shut, more than his palms were sweating.

"Hi," Carly said.

"Hi," was all he could manage to answer. Then he shook his head. Now he understood why her brothers had been so protective. It was a wonder they hadn't wrapped her in a robe and thrown a veil over her face.

Carly carried the conversation during the brief trip to Mayor Goodman's house. Russ was still trying to deal with the change in her. He was very careful not to touch her, because once he did, he knew he wouldn't stop until she'd eased the ache in his loins. He pulled the car to a stop and took a fortifying breath before he got out and led Carly up the walkway.

With a pained smile on her face, Janet Goodman answered the door of the two-story home. A chorus of howls started up as soon as they walked through the door.

"The twins are teething, and my daughter went out on her first date," Janet explained.

"So you lost your baby-sitter," Carly concluded.

"I need another shirt," Sam yelled from upstairs. "Robbie drooled all over this one."

"Coming," Janet called, then she turned back to Russ and Carly. "Please forgive me, but—"

Another chorus of howls broke out.

"Could I check on the boys?" Carly asked. "I haven't seen them in a long time."

Relief and gratitude crossed Janet's face. "Oh, would you please? I know they'll settle down soon. Just make sure you put on a smock so they don't ruin that lovely dress."

The doorbell rang.

"And Russ, would you please get that? I'll be down in just a minute. Help yourself to the bar and the appetizers in the parlor." Janet disappeared up the stairs.

Carly and Russ looked at each other and laughed.

"I, uh, guess I'll see you later," Carly said, wishing he would touch her, wishing she could touch him. He'd seemed so remote since they'd left her apartment.

The doorbell rang again, and Russ nodded.

Carly went up the stairs.

"Don't stay too long," Russ called after her in a low voice that stopped her midstep. "I might have to come get you."

There was something faintly predatory in his tone. It sent a shiver up her spine and brought a warmth to her skin. She wondered what it would be like to have Russ Bradford *get her*.

After fifteen minutes of patting Ronnie and jiggling Robbie, the twins miraculously fell asleep.

When she made her way into the dining room, Janet and Sam greeted her with welcoming smiles. "You must be a miracle worker," Sam said. "I'd been rocking those boys for a half hour."

"They were just tired," Carly said. She'd felt like curling up in that rocking chair herself. Last night, she'd stayed up a good part of the night stuffing envelopes with her new brochures.

"Wine?" Russ came to her side and offered her a glass.

He casually wrapped an arm around her waist, and she leaned closer to him. "Thanks," she murmured. She stole a glance at him and noticed his gaze rested on her bare shoulder. A tiny thrill raced through her, and she gave in to the urge to tease him the way he did her.

"Hungry, Russ?" Carly asked in a low, seductive voice.

His gaze shot up to her eyes, probing and hot. "Very," he growled and tightened his hold on her.

This tarnishing business may not be so difficult after all, Carly thought.

After the meal, the other guests left while Russ and Sam discussed Beulah County's upcoming carnival. Janet showed Carly pictures of the twins' christening. For the first time in a long time, Carly felt a twinge of longing over the idea of having a family. Janet and Sam seemed so happy.

Carly wrinkled her brow, remembering her grueling accelerated college program that had left no time for a social life. After that, she'd inherited *Matilda's Dream* and immersed herself in making it a thriving enterprise.

Glancing at Russ, she wondered if she was missing out on something important. Of course, everybody knew Russ would never settle down. She would have to remember that. While he might be a good choice for tarnishing a woman's reputation, he'd be horrible at marriage.

Russ looked up just then, and held her gaze. That lazy smile slowly eased up the corners of his mouth. With his eyes still on her, he said to Sam, "I think it's time for us to go. Thanks for having us, Sam."

After complimenting Janet on the meal, Carly and Russ stepped into the humid night. Clouds covered the moon in streaks of dark blue, muting the light. Crickets chirped in the lawn.

Russ guided her down the walk with a firm, warm hand on her waist. Coupled with the wine, his nearness made her pleasantly dizzy.

"I really like them," Carly said.

"Yeah," Russ agreed, then chuckled. "Janet looked a little frazzled when we got there."

"She had to work hard to put on that welcoming smile."

"The earring was what I noticed," Russ said and chuckled again. "She was wearing only one."

His low, deep voice so close to her made the blood bubble through her veins like champagne. Russ's car was only a few steps away, and Carly felt reluctant to leave the evening behind. She sighed.

"Tired?" he asked.

She shrugged.

"It was nice of you to help Janet with the twins."

"They're cute. Robbie's got dimples." She looked up at Russ. The streetlight was broken, so his face was all hard planes and shadows. She touched his cheek.

Her feather-light touch stopped him in his tracks.

"Did you ever have dimples, Russ?" Carly asked and frowned. "I can't remember."

Thirsty for her touch, he shook his head. "No, but you did," he whispered.

"Not anymore," Carly whispered back.

Her eyes were as blue-black as the night, and she was looking at him in a womanly wanting way. He turned her in his arms, slightly, slowly, wondering if and when she'd pull away. To his surprise, she moved closer. Her fragrance wove its way around his mind, stealing his sense. Her breasts were one deep breath away from his chest. It would only take one step to feel her legs brushing against his tensed and waiting thighs.

Her lids lowered, hiding her eyes from his. Still her hand remained soft and caressing on his cheek.

"Russ, I don't really care whether you had dimples or not. I just wanted an excuse to touch you," Carly said in a voice so low, he almost couldn't hear her.

His heart turned over. He took a deep breath, and she closed the miniscule gap between them.

"Know what I wish now?"

"What?" he asked, keeping his voice quiet, not wanting to disturb the magic of her closeness.

Carly looked up at him then and moved her hand behind his neck. The gesture was unmistakable. She pulled his head gently toward hers.

"I wish I knew what your mouth felt like," she said in a husky voice.

His heart somersaulted, and his blood roared in his ears. He'd always considered himself a man with superior self-control, but when she tentatively touched her lips to his, he lost it all.

His hands clenched around her forearms. There would be bruises tomorrow. He took her supple mouth with the passion of a man who'd waited too long. He thrust his tongue past her parted lips, wanting to possess her body, mind, and soul with the kiss.

When she gave a soft little moan, he checked himself and gentled, letting her explore. With a mix of excruciating pain and pleasure, he responded to her sweet probes, molding her body to his. She pushed her fingers through his hair.

He ran his restless hands up and down that sanity-robbing dress of hers, stopping just short of her breasts. When she rubbed against him, he groaned and gave up on restraint and felt the shape of one plump breast in his hand.

"Oh," Carly murmured against his open mouth. She edged her lips away, gasping for air. Her body hummed as if she'd been caught in an electrical storm. Still stroking her peaked breast, he kissed her neck and bare shoulder.

"You could push a man straight over the edge," he muttered.

She could feel his hardness pressing against her. She could hear the desire in his voice. The knowledge made her blood pool low in her abdomen.

His breathing harsh and unsteady, Russ slipped his hand to her back. He pulled her to him, as close as they could get, clothed, under the mayor's broken streetlight.

They stood that way for several moments until finally sanity returned. With reluctance and care, he separated their bodies and looked into her dazed eyes. "Well, did you get your wish?"

He watched Carly's gaze fall to his mouth. He felt the burning begin again and shook his head. If he kissed her again, he'd have a hard time not ripping that little dress off. Somehow, he managed to unlock the car and help her into it.

With jerky movements, he started the car and put it into gear.

"Russ," Carly began, "know what I wish now?"

A strangled laugh bubbled from his throat. "Carly."

"What?"

"Shut up."

She did.

Russ spent the rest of the drive to her apartment wondering how to subdue the firecracker in his passenger seat without completely dousing the flame. He hadn't counted on her initiating anything between them. *This wasn't part of his plan.*

He knew it was too early to take her to bed. If he'd wanted her just for the night, he wouldn't hesitate. She was ready. Lord knew, he was ready. That she'd tempted him beyond his self-control made him uneasy.

Grimly, he drummed his fingers on the steering wheel, recalling the other time he'd given his emotions free rein. Talk about a nightmare. This head-over-heels business was for the birds, Russ thought, stifling a snort. He'd arrived at his decision to marry Carly after months of careful evaluation, and it comforted him to know he wasn't selecting a mate based on emotional hogwash.

Carly's trust was critical, however, and a too-early loving could mess that up. Other issues needed to be settled first. They needed to establish themselves as a couple. He wanted her to confide in him, to believe in him. Russ resolved to keep the logical sequence firmly in his mind.

Letting out a long breath, he pulled the car to a stop and turned to face her. The woman was a vixen. She was so sexy with her mussed hair and swollen lips. She was a provocative invitation to insanity and ecstasy.

She was also asleep.

There was a pleasurable irony to this situation, he realized, as he took her sleeping form into his arms and carried her up the steps to her apartment. She was dead to the world. It made him wonder what time she'd been getting to bed.

He shifted her weight slightly to pull the key from her white purse. When she started to fall, he jammed the key into the lock.

After shoving the door open, he paused to let his eyes adjust to the pitch darkness.

Out of nowhere a fist struck his jaw. He shouted at the pain. Carly jerked awake and screamed. Still reeling from the blow, Russ grabbed the door and tried to shove her outside in a protective maneuver.

The door slammed against the jamb, trapping his hand. Russ cursed, pushing Carly to the side, kicking and striking at two indistinct forms.

He felt the satisfying impact of his fist against flesh. He heard a grunt of pain. His foot connected with an animate object. A yelp followed. Then a very familiar voice growled, "What are you doing with my sister, you sonova—"

"Troy!" Russ shouted. He'd thought they were burglars or worse.

Carly hit the lights and stared down at her oldest and youngest brothers. They lay sprawled on the floor with dumbstruck, then sheepish expressions on their faces. Daniel was rubbing his shin, while Troy gingerly felt his eye.

With an audible wince, Russ pulled his hand from the doorway. "I'm not sure I want to know what this is all about," he said, then looked at Carly. "I need some ice."

Gritting her teeth, she motioned toward the kitchen. "In there." Extreme embarrassment fueled her anger. She turned her furious gaze on her brothers.

"Aw, hell," Daniel said, covering his face.

"You're ten years older than I am," Carly said. "You should know better. How'd you get in?"

"Your next-door neighbor let us in. I know. I know. I was at loose ends, and Troy suggested driving by to check on you." He shrugged. "It was habit."

"One you need to break," she said emphatically. Daniel had always been the steady, even-tempered leader. Carly thought he'd seemed restless lately. "Get a life of your own."

"Now, hold on, Carly." Troy shuffled to his feet. "How were we supposed to know you were out with Russ?"

"You don't have to know," she shrieked. "I'm twenty-three years old."

"Mama would turn over in her grave if she saw you in that dress," Troy continued, ignoring her protests.

"Then shall I strip it off and take a walk down Main Street?" Carly asked vehemently.

Daniel muttered a barnyard curse.

Troy remained uncharacteristically silent.

Shaking with fury, she pressed her hands against her heated face. "Am I going to have to move out of town to get some space?"

Russ came up from behind and placed a placating hand on her shoulder. "Now, Carly, don't be rash."

She stiffened at his tone.

"Your brothers are a little misguided, but they lo—"

She jerked away. "Don't you dare tell me what to do."

Suddenly it was all too much. The way her brothers constantly intruded into her life, the way Russ had maneuvered her into escorting him this summer, the damning way she'd gotten distracted from her goal of buying out her brothers.

The last one was the worst. With stunning clarity, Carly realized she'd allowed one more manipulating male to get in her way. And she'd invited Russ to do far more than kiss her tonight.

She felt like a fool.

Taking a deep breath, she looked at the three men responsible for her present humiliation. Without a word, she opened the door. Her meaning was perfectly clear.

Daniel left first, then Troy.

Russ stopped in front of her and hesitated.

The hesitation nearly undid her. She wanted to ask about his hand. She wanted to look at him, but she was afraid of what she'd see. If it was concern, the tightly held tears would fall and she'd feel foolish again.

She bit her lip hard and turned away.

He stood close enough for her to feel his heavy sigh against her forehead. "I'll talk to you later," he said in a low voice before he left.

As if from a distance, she heard the hollow sound of his footsteps down the hall. And she found, to her dismay, that those tightly held tears had already begun to fall down her cheeks.

Four

Russ gingerly crunched down on the crisp, extra brown toast and grimaced. He threw the charred bread into the trash and sat down. It wasn't worth the effort it took to eat it, he thought as he leaned back in the oak kitchen chair. For a moment he wondered if marriage to Carly was worth all this trouble. Between his sore jaw, bruised hand, and injured ego, he felt in need of rehabilitative therapy.

He scowled when he remembered the previous evening. Carly had been furious, and he supposed she had a right. Still her brothers' protective demonstration would result in a major setback in his plans. He frowned at the cheerful yellow wallpaper covering his kitchen wall.

Now how the hell was he supposed to get things back on track? He plopped his chin into his hand. Searing pain immediately shot through his jaw. He let out a string of curses. At the same moment, the doorbell rang. Russ glowered at the door, praying his visitor would be someone on whom he could vent his frustration. It might be one of his employees, he realized. But he was in a nasty mood. With a rough growl, he stalked to the door and jerked it open.

There she stood. The object of his complete mental, physical, and sexual frustration. Russ considered throwing her over his shoulder and hauling her into his bedroom. That would solve one of his problems. And Carly would just *love* the male domination bit, the sane part of his mind sarcastically reminded him.

He hadn't uttered a word of greeting, and he noticed she was starting to chew on her bottom lip. He narrowed his eyes. She shifted once, then again. Her nervousness mollified him enough to speak. "Yeah."

She swallowed. "I, uh, I thought I'd better check and see how you're doing." She took her hands from her pockets and gestured toward him. "You know, your jaw and your hand."

"I'm fine," he said, letting her squirm.

"Oh, well." She gave a weak smile and shrugged. "I'm glad. If you don't need anything, I'll just—"

"Need anything?" Russ interrupted.

"Yes. I didn't know if you'd need any help today with your hand. And since it was my brothers who . . ."

"Slammed the door on my hand and nearly cracked my jaw," Russ supplied.

Carly winced. "Yes. I'm sorry, Russ. I was so angry with them, and I shouldn't have taken it out on you."

Her confession soothed his grouchiness. Russ relaxed slightly. "It's okay. You want to come in?"

She nodded and walked through the doorway. She wrinkled her nose. "Burned your toast?"

"Yeah."

She turned around and took a step closer to him, studying his jaw. "Your right jaw looks like a chipmunk's."

"Thank you," he said dryly.

She smiled and lifted his bruised hand, gently studying the swelling and discoloration. "Can I fix you some breakfast, something soft like eggs and grits?"

"Sounds good." He liked the sensation of her soft hands on his. In fact, he wouldn't mind if she extended the caress to his entire body.

"You think it would help if I bandaged this?" Carly asked, a frown creasing her brow.

"Probably wouldn't hurt." Russ felt like a first grader trying to monopolize the teacher's attention. He sat down at the oak kitchen table and directed her to the first-aid kit. She wore a pair of faded denims that molded to her rear end in a tantalizing way. Her blue T-shirt should have been boring, but Carly had neglected to wear a bra. Russ cleared his throat and shook his head.

Carly scooted the chair closer to Russ and deftly wound the bandage around his swollen hand. "There," she said when she finished. She tried, unsuccessfully, to keep her eyes above his neck. His striped cotton shirt was completely unbuttoned, offering an engrossing view of his chest and flat belly. His chest hair was curly, she noticed. She also noticed the way it arrowed down the center of his stomach to his navel. She wondered if it felt soft or crisp.

Carly deliberately brought her gaze back at his face. "Did you have problems buttoning your shirt?" She hoped he would take the hint and cover up before she did something embarrassing like start drooling.

"Yeah, would you mind doing it for me?"

Carly blinked. "Do what?"

"Button my shirt."

Her heart squeezed like a giant fist. He might as well have asked her to lay on top of him. Couldn't he hear her uneven breathing? Did he have any idea how difficult this was for her? She searched his eyes, but his lowered lids hid any expression from her.

Carly gritted her teeth in determination. "Okay." She lifted her hands, facing her first major decision. Should she start at the top or the bottom? He was sitting, and the shirttails rested on either side of his crotch. Which, of course, meant she'd be touching his crotch when she buttoned it. Undiluted panic raced through her.

The top. Definitely the top. Biting her lip, she buttoned the top button and the second, then looked at Russ's brown eyes. They were so sexy and seductive, she could have been unbuttoning his shirt instead of buttoning it. Carly turned back to her task and discovered that his chest hair was soft. She would have loved to run her fingers through it. She managed to abstain, but it cost her. With each successive button, her mouth grew drier. It may have been her imagination, but it seemed his breathing quickened too. When she reached the third button from the bottom, she stopped, her mouth drier than the Sahara. "I, uh . . ."

"Thanks," Russ said.

Carly smiled in relief.

"Want to tuck it in?"

Her head snapped up, catching the devil's glint in his eyes. Funny, his voice had sounded dead serious. She laughed weakly. "I think I'll fix those eggs."

She prepared and served his breakfast, chatting about the farm and anything else that came to mind as he ate. "I envy this kitchen. The Italian tile is gorgeous. And that convection oven is a dream." She admired the way he'd achieved a fresh, clean room without losing the masculine edge. The golden oak table, chairs, and cabinets added warmth and depth.

"You can use it anytime. Especially if you'll undo these top two buttons. I'm about to choke." Russ gave a fake cough.

Carly rolled her eyes and quickly performed the task. "You should have told me. What do you need to do now?"

Russ leaned back and stretched. "Scare off some cormorants."

Carly frowned in confusion. "But we don't usually see them until September."

Russ shrugged. "I know. It must be a crazy flock. Either way, they can catch as many as twenty-three catfish an hour, and once they get started it only gets worse. I've got to move pop-up scarecrows and shoot flare pistols today."

"Do you want some help?"

"Sure. But I'd also like to know what you think about last night." His gaze was serious and intent.

"I'm still mad at Troy and Daniel, but I'll get over it."

"And about what happened before that?"

Feeling uneasy, Carly wiped the counters with a damp sponge. "I enjoyed the Goodmans. They're great people."

"What about my dimples?"

"You don't have dimples."

"What about my mouth?"

Her breath hung in her throat. The memory of his mouth on hers brought a rush of excitement that took her like a tidal wave. She fought against it. "C'mon Russ," she said with forced lightness. "You know how it was. Just a little too much wine and curiosity." She looked up then, begging him with her eyes not to push the subject.

Russ just raised a skeptical eyebrow. He rose and stuffed his shirt into his jeans. Carly remembered she could have had that job, and wanted to kick herself for thinking it.

"Let's go," Russ said.

"But the dishes—"

"—will go in the dishwasher. Let's go."

A few minutes later, they were riding down a bumpy dirt road surrounding large ponds. While the sun shone on the water, birds sang out their various morning calls and Russ's hounds barked a welcome. It was warm already. She lowered the window to let in the breeze. It had been a while since she'd been out to Russ's farm and even longer since she'd taken a ride in his old pickup truck.

Carly wasn't sure why she'd come this morning. Part of it was that she'd felt unreasonably guilty about how her brothers had injured Russ. He'd been an innocent party. As innocent as Russ Bradford could be, she thought wryly as she glanced at him.

Part of it stemmed from her confusion over their relationship. Whatever happened between them, Carly didn't want to lose Russ's friendship. Last night she had blamed Russ for distracting her, when in fact, she was responsible. She knew she was unbearably attracted to him, but she also knew she needed to rein in those feelings. They would pass. She was sure of it.

"What are you going to do about Daniel and Troy?" Russ asked as he stopped the truck.

"Now, that's a leading question. I don't know what to do with Troy, but Daniel . . ."

"Daniel?"

"I think what Daniel needs is a good woman."

Russ grinned. "Got anyone in mind?"

"As a matter of fact, I do." She shoved open the truck door. "My assistant Sara."

They walked through the tall grass to where Russ began to set up a pop-up scarecrow. He held it while she hammered it into the ground.

"Do you think he'll go for it?" Carly asked.

"He'll fight it every inch of the way, but he'll give in at the end. It's time for him to settle down."

Carly did a double take. "I'm surprised to hear that from you, the eternal rogue."

"Why? Just about every man eventually wants to have a wife and kids."

Carly gave the pop-up one last whack. "Not you." She took another look at the scarecrow and shook her head at the lime-green pants and orange shirt. "His clothes don't match."

"We're not trying to make a fashion statement here. They're supposed to wear bright colors." He pulled her along beside him. "Come on. We don't have all day. Now, about Troy?"

Carly joined Russ in the truck. It was so nice being with him this way that she wanted to confide in him. "I don't have anyone picked out for Troy." Carly studied Russ. She liked the way he listened to her. He took her seriously when others didn't. "Can you keep this confidential?"

His gaze flickered over her. "Sure."

She took a deep breath. "I want to buy my brothers' shares in *Matilda's Dream* this fall. I'm living on a shoestring budget and working extra hard this summer. I hope to get a loan for anything I can't cover."

Russ whistled. "Have you got much saved?"

Carly pushed her hand through her hair in exasperation. "Not enough. That's what worries me. And if I don't get ownership by fall, I might have to do something desperate."

"Like what?" Russ asked, not liking the sound of this.

"I don't know." Carly shrugged her shoulders restlessly. "Sell out and move to Memphis or Nashville."

Her words struck hard and fast. He silently absorbed the blow. In his most neutral voice, and because he had to know, he asked, "Is that what you want?"

"No."

Her quick response instantly eased him. Russ let out a deep breath.

Carly gazed at him, her eyes pleading for understanding. "I think it might be easier for them to let go if I move." Her voice caught. "I need something of my own."

Russ saw the moisture in her eyes and felt a twisting in his insides. He'd always hated to see Carly in pain. Without a second thought, he hauled her over the gearshift and into his lap. He wrapped her in a deep, affectionate hug.

"Oh, Russ," she said, and the tears began to flow.

"Hush," he murmured, rubbing the silk of her hair. "It will all work out, Carly. Time changes everything. Who knows? By the end of summer, your brothers might get married and start their own families."

"Hah." Carly rubbed her wet cheeks with the back of her hands. "The likelihood of them getting married is the same as it is for me. Zero."

Russ ground his teeth. "You don't know that. You watch and see. Things could turn around for you in a big way this summer." He hitched her chin upward with his finger. "Just don't go planning any big moves to Memphis or Nashville. I'd pine away without you here in Beulah."

Carly smiled slowly. Then she chuckled. Russ always managed to make her laugh. "I've never seen you lacking for female consolation."

"Then maybe you haven't looked close enough," he said quietly and set her back in her seat.

She immediately missed his warmth. She studied him carefully. His amber eyes held no hint of teasing. He started the truck, and Carly thought about Russ, wondering if she was wrong about him. He might be a rogue, but she didn't have a better friend. He was tough, but extraordinarily kind. Was there something inside him that longed for one true love and a peaceful, settled life? Remembering his brief marriage and all the women since, Carly shook her head. If he'd really wanted to settle down, he'd had a dozen opportunities.

With good-natured bickering, they finished setting up the scarecrows. She swatted him when he lamented her puny biceps. They caught sight of a cormorant, its black body flying in a silent V. The bird did a surface dive, preparing to catch a fish. Russ shot off a flare, and the bird quickly veered up and away.

They drove back to his house then. In spite of the work waiting for her at home, she found herself reluctant to go.

Russ leaned against the truck. "No cruises tonight?"

"No. Sunday nights are slow, so I try to catch up on paperwork and bookkeeping." Carly stretched. "I must be out of shape. I'll probably be sore tomorrow."

His gaze flicked over her, making her feel unclothed. Her stomach fluttered.

"Want a massage?"

Lord. How did he manage to make her feel as though she were stuck on the top of a Ferris wheel? "You have only one good hand," she reminded him.

"But it's very good."

Her heart thumped in her chest. She'd just bet his hand was very good. Good enough to send a woman into permanent oblivious ecstasy.

Russ moved closer. She instinctively stepped backward and bumped into the truck. Russ put his hand on her shoulder, and she was trapped by the look in his eyes.

"Last night you said you wished you knew what my mouth felt like. Today you say it was just too much wine and too much curiosity. Well, I haven't had a sip of wine, and I gotta tell you I'm burning up with curiosity."

He lowered his head, and her breath stopped. His lips grazed hers once, twice, then settled warmly against her mouth. His tongue toyed with her while his thumb began a tantalizing motion on her throat.

She felt a sinking sensation so strong, she clutched his shoulders, needing something solid to hold on to. Russ muttered her name against her lips, then slid his hand down her neck. He brushed his fingers over her breast, missing the nipple that strained against her T-shirt for his attention.

Carly's breasts ached. As if he'd read her mind, he flicked his thumb over her puckered nipple. She closed her eyes. His touch seemed to make the wanting spread deeper. He nuzzled her head, inviting her to see the hunger in his eyes. In a sexy kind of lethargy, Carly looked up and felt a disconcerting weakness in her knees. She stiffened them.

Russ's hands slid to her waist. He pulled the shirt from her jeans. Reaching down, he kissed her thoroughly as he raised the bottom of her shirt inch by devastating inch until her breasts were bared. He molded a naked, swollen breast with one of his callused hands and pressed his hard thighs against her. Her knees buckled.

"Oh," she gasped, her mouth open against his.

Wrapping his hands around her waist, he propped her on the hood of the truck, then moved between her thighs. Carly stared into his eyes, unable to look away.

"Wrap your legs around me," he said.

Carly began to tremble. "What?"

He didn't repeat himself. He just lifted her legs around his waist so that his hardness nudged her. If they were naked, she thought, he'd be inside her. Her mouth went dry.

His gaze held hers until finally he lowered his eyes to her breasts. Carly had never felt more beautiful or more erotically aware than she did now with the noonday sun beating down on her and Russ Bradford's mouth lowering to her tight, sensitive nipples. His tongue and teeth teased her deliciously. When he sucked her breast deep into his mouth, she arched her back. The heaviness in her intensified, and she felt a moist melting sensation where his erection rubbed against her.

He switched breasts, and Carly moaned in frustration. She wished she were naked. She wished he were naked.

She wished he were inside her.

"Russ," she cried, tangling her fingers in his dark red hair.

Russ looked up and saw the flush of arousal on

her face. Leaning forward, he kept his eyes open as he licked her lips with his tongue. His gaze traveled from her mouth to her nipples, glistening from his ministrations. "You're wet," he muttered with approval. Carly's eyes were hazy with desire. His loins were ready to burst from the intensity of his arousal. He moved his hands to the button of her jeans and tugged.

Lost in the moment, he barely heard anything but Carly's soft gasp and moan. A bunch of dogs barked in the distance. At first the sound didn't penetrate his sensual fog. Finally, Russ comprehended it. He blinked and glanced around, shaking his head. He stopped fooling with the button of her jeans and lifted his hands from her body.

In that instant, his eyes changed. Carly saw the moment he realized the precariousness of their situation. He cursed and closed his eyes. Carly stiffened, feeling an instant surge of shame. With bare breasts and spread thighs she must appear as she was, totally wanton. Awkward and confused, she pulled her hands from his hair and fumbled with her shirt. Russ stopped her with a grip of steel.

Carly looked away, unwilling to reveal her feelings. She knew her eyes wouldn't hide a thing, and there was no reasonable explanation for her actions. Except, perhaps temporary insanity.

"Don't look away," he pleaded roughly. "Please don't look away. Come on, baby," he coaxed, tenderly guiding her chin.

She opened her eyes and saw the honest, savage need in his and didn't feel quite so humiliated anymore.

"Talk to me," Russ whispered.

"I don't know what to say." She looked at him, still

feeling his pulsating hardness pressed against her. "Why did you stop?"

Russ groaned and lowered her shirt with unsteady hands. "I was so far gone, I was ready to take you on the hood of this pickup truck, Carly." He kissed her mouth, then gave a wry grin. "That's not exactly the best place for a first-timer to shed her . . ."

"Virginity," she finished bluntly. She drew back from him. "Did it show that much?"

His gaze darkened. "Don't even think it."

Feeling the threat of tears, Carly blinked fiercely and looked away. She saw a cardinal perching on the large oak tree. "Does it bother you that I'm a virgin?" She heard the hoarseness in her voice, but couldn't do a thing about it. Her emotions were in an uproar.

Russ took her palm and pressed it against his throbbing hardness. "Look at me."

Carly fought against the seductive huskiness in his voice. She tried to pull back her hand, but he held firm. She finally looked at him.

"Feel me, Carly." His eyes blazed with arousal as he molded her hand around him.

He was hot and hard as steel, and she found herself resenting the jeans he wore. She wanted to touch him there, where he was most vulnerable, most needy, and most male.

"I'll probably be in this state for the rest of the day." He moved her hand in a stroking motion and let out a long hiss of breath. "I think it's fair to say I'm gonna be *bothered* until we go to bed."

Russ didn't hide the extent of his desire for her. His need was honest and irresistibly compelling, and she was amazed at the power she seemed to hold over him. He was such a big, powerful man.

With visible reluctance, he pulled her hand from

his jeans and pressed his lips to her palm. "You name the time, lady," he said. "But think it over, because one time isn't going to do it for me. One night won't do it."

Carly heard the warning in his voice. She looked at him with his ruffled auburn hair glinting in the sun, his eyes completely serious. This was not the Russ from her childhood. This was the man. And he wanted her badly.

The image of long, hot nights, cool, cotton sheets, and tangled bodies filled her mind. A breathtaking excitement seized her. This would be no easy coupling, she realized. It would be hot and hard and strong like Russ. And God help her, she didn't know how to handle it.

Carly made it home without wrecking the car. Even though she turned the air conditioner on high (and closed all the windows,) she was still hot by the time she climbed the steps to her apartment. She was almost as stunned by Russ as she was by her own feelings. The only element in this entire situation that comforted her was the fact that Russ had given her ultimate control. "You name the time," he'd said. Carly knew she wasn't ready. Physically, yes. Emotionally, no.

When she thought about making love with Russ, her chest tightened with apprehension. Or was it anticipation? She went into her apartment and slammed the door behind her. Maybe she should just do it and get it over with, she thought irritably as she stomped to the bathroom to run a cool bath. Maybe if she did it, her curiosity would be satisfied.

She might even be disappointed, she thought doubt-fully.

Maybe she'd fall madly in love with Russ and make a complete fool of herself.

What would happen to their friendship afterward? Carly threw some bath salts into the tub. The nature of their friendship had changed, she admitted. Part of her longed for the uncomplicated relationship she used to share with Russ. In spite of the fact that he'd been best friends with her brothers, she'd grown to count on him as an ally.

She swirled the water around with her fingers and sighed. Something inside her had changed irrevoca-bly. The feeling was so intense, it frightened her. Would she ever be able to look at Russ again and not feel a quickening inside her? And what if this wasn't just lust? she asked herself in horror.

One thing at a time. The lust was overwhelming enough without her worrying about other more se-rious possibilities. The question, she knew, was if—or when? The idea of actually going through with it brought a rush of heat to her entire body. She groaned, then stripped off her clothes and tried to ignore the way she still tingled from Russ's touch. She stepped into the tub and completely immersed herself in the cool, fragrant water in hopes of erasing Russ's devastating effect on her. Closing her eyes, she decided she simply wasn't ready to decide.

After a busy week, Carly sat in her riverboat, listening to her brothers' arguments, and wondered if they had any seats available on the next space shuttle.

Daniel shook his head. "I don't like the second

guy's voice. And if I don't like it, you know the customers won't either."

Troy argued. "He wasn't as bad as the first one."

Carly pinched the bridge of her nose. She felt a headache coming on. They were discussing the wait-staff applicants. Her brothers had tiptoed around their apologies to Carly, then proceeded to interfere with business instead of her social life. She didn't know which was worse.

"Which do you like better, Carly?" Garth asked.

Carly blinked. It was the first time she'd been asked. "I like them both, but we need a tenor if they're going to do four-part harmony."

Troy opened his mouth to argue.

"We need another male waiter ready by next weekend," she interjected before he could get started. "I'll give you five minutes to reach a decision. I've got too much to do to get ready for those travel agents coming next week."

"And that's another thing," Troy said. "I still don't think you oughta be giving all those people a complimentary cruise. How do you know they're gonna send any business your way?"

Carly pressed her lips together. Troy made a valid point. She should take a harder line on offering reduced rates, except with charities. But her instincts rebelled at the notion, and she refused to get off track. She glanced at her watch. "Four minutes."

She leaned back, mentally extricating herself from the argument.

"How's Russ?" Garth asked.

"I haven't talked to him lately, but I think his hand should be better by now."

Garth narrowed his eyes. "He hasn't called you?"

Carly shifted in her seat. Garth didn't intrude as

much as her other brothers. He was quiet, but extremely perceptive. He always remembered her birthday and sent Carly her favorite flowers. She'd heard more than one woman gush over his dark, brooding good looks. At the moment, however, Carly found his perceptiveness and attention to detail unnerving.

"Well, you know I've been real busy this week," Carly said. "He might have left a message or two." Or three or four, she thought. Her busyness was the superficial reason she hadn't returned his calls. Her confusion was the deeper reason.

"We've decided," Daniel announced. "Take the first guy on a trial basis."

Troy grumbled, "If I can find somebody else, I'll send him over."

Carly smiled in relief. "There. I knew you could come to some kind of agreement. I'll call the applicant tomorrow." She stood and took Daniel by the arm and led him to the door. "Thanks for coming. Go ahead and set up your dates for the travel agents' cruise."

Troy and Garth automatically shuffled behind Daniel.

"Who's your date?" Garth asked as Carly opened the door.

"No one. I'll be too busy taking care of the guests."

"What about Russ?" Garth continued.

Carly inhaled quickly.

Daniel laughed. "Russ is just relying on Carly for camouflage this summer. The Ladies Auxiliary is after him."

Garth frowned. "Is that what he said?"

"Hell, yes," Troy answered. "He knows we wouldn't let him near Carly."

"Don't stay out long, Carly," Daniel reminded her.

Carly reached up and kissed him on the cheek. "Same to you. Good night." She gave a quick peck to her other brothers and tried to ignore the thoughtful expression on Garth's face.

After closing the door behind them, she walked back in the room and sank into a chair. It was just one more reason why an affair with Russ would never work. Her brothers were worse than the FBI. They'd find out and send her to a convent. Russ's fate would be easier. They'd just shoot him.

Her elbows planted on the table, Carly rested her head on her hands and closed her eyes. Lord help her, what was she going to do? At the same time that she'd avoided Russ, she'd missed him. What a mess. She could use a fairy godmother right now, she thought. Or at least a friend.

As if her secret wish had been granted, she heard a familiar low voice. "Rough week, lady?"

Four cups of coffee injected into her veins couldn't have had a more pronounced effect on her system. Carly jerked upright, wondering if she was having delusions.

There he stood, leaning against the dark wooden wall. He came complete with black T-shirt and tight, worn jeans that celebrated maleness in a way that Chippendales dancers could only wish for. His mouth turned up in a thigh-melting smile while his caramel eyes glinted with gentle humor.

Her heart beat an unsteady rhythm against her chest. When he pushed away from the wall and strolled toward her, Carly scrambled to her feet.

"I, uh, I didn't know you were coming tonight." Carly bit her clumsy tongue.

"I left a message with Sara. As a matter of fact, I left five messages with Sara."

Carly winced. "I've been really busy this week, between hiring new waitstaff and getting ready for those travel agents." She swallowed and stood. "Can I get you something to drink?"

"Hold on." Russ caught her arm. His eyebrows furrowed as he studied her face. "Carly, you're trembling! What's wrong?"

"I told you," she insisted with a wavery voice. "I'm busy." She hated this out-of-control feeling she had.

"Then tell me what I can do to help."

She took a deep, calming breath. "For starters, you can let go of my arm."

She saw surprise, a flash of hurt. Then his face closed up. He dropped her arm. "Okay."

He shoved his hands into his pockets and watched her. "You want to tell me what's going on?"

Carly ran a hand through her hair. She was so upset, she felt like crying, but there was no logical reason for it. "I don't know how to act around you anymore, Russ. This stuff between us has happened so quickly. One day we're friends; the next I'm practically making love to you on top of your pickup truck." She lifted her hands in confusion.

Russ's gaze was gentle and understanding. He stepped forward and reached out his hand. "I told you, you name the—"

Carly backed away, stumbling over her chair. It turned over and fell to the floor with a loud bang.

Russ stared at her as if she'd lost her mind.

Carly was pretty sure that's exactly what she'd done.

Five

"I'm not gonna jump you," Russ finally said.

"I know," Carly retorted. She jerked the chair up and scooted it under the table. Feeling uncomfortable, she crossed her arms over her chest. "I'm not sure about all this. I think it might be better—if you didn't . . ." Her voice faltered when she saw the intent expression in his eyes.

"If I didn't what?"

"Touch me." Carly let out a frustrated sigh. She knew she was overreacting, and she felt like an idiot. But when Russ touched her, she could practically smell the smoke. And the fire came from inside her.

"Why?"

She should have known he would ask why. "Well, it complicates things. It could mess up our friendship. It makes me feel confused." *It makes me hot.*

With a knowing light in his eyes, Russ nodded. "You're worried about losing our friendship?"

"Yes," she breathed, feeling a surge of relief. He understood.

"We'll always be friends, Carly. No matter what else happens between us. I can promise you that." He flicked his gaze over her quickly. "I can also promise you that I won't touch you unless I ask you first and that I'll stop when you ask me to." He moved closer and held his hands out by his sides, signaling that he was playing by her rules. "But stopping the touching won't stop the wanting."

It has to, she thought desperately. She needed to get a grip on this. She needed to gain some perspective, bring this insanity under control. Carly cleared her throat. "Let's just try it."

"Okay." His face was serious except for the devil's glint in his eyes. "But this goes completely against my nature. I'm not sure you know how *hard* this is gonna be."

Carly smiled in spite of her inner tension. "Yeah," she said dryly. "Just think of it as a character-building experience, Russ."

He chuckled. "You're tough."

"Between you and my brothers, I've got to be." She glanced at her watch and exclaimed over the time. "I need to close up and get home."

Russ noted the way she grouped him with her brothers. It irritated him. He'd have to fix that later. Right now, he had to make sure she didn't slip away completely. "I wanted to remind you about Games Day for the hospital on Saturday." She looked as though she'd forgotten. That further irritated him. "Is there a problem?"

"No," Carly assured him quickly and gave a self-deprecating smile. "I just can't seem to hold anything in my brain for more than a few minutes lately. I'll make sure everything's covered."

"Good. I'll pick you up around eleven o'clock." His

gaze fell to her breasts, and he shook his head. "If you want me to stick to this no-touch rule, you'd better wear a bra."

Her eyes rounded, and she gave a choky laugh. "Anything else?"

Russ grinned slowly. "Nah. I'd suggest a paper bag, but it wouldn't slow me down." He blew her a kiss. "See you Saturday."

Carly watched him swagger from the room. She withheld her groan for all of three seconds.

It looked as though nearly everyone in town showed up for Games Day, Carly thought. She ought to be able to keep her senses in this innocuous situation. Russ wouldn't be able to weave his enticing spell over her in George Killion's fallow pasture full of men, women, and children. Beulah County wanted their emergency room better equipped, and the residents believed people shelled out money more readily when fun and food were offered.

Carly heard a yelp and looked at the dunking booth. "Looks like Mayor Goodman got it," she said to Russ.

He grinned. "Yeah. It's hot so he probably doesn't mind too much."

She saw a couple of kids with blue cotton candy and smelled catfish frying. "Did you donate the fish again?"

He nodded, then looked down at a piece of paper in his hand. "We're supposed to lead the wheelbarrow race for the first hour, then the three-legged relay. We have to demonstrate correct racing positions and award the ribbons. Then we finish up with the tug-of-war over the creek." He clicked his tongue.

"Let's get going. Wheelbarrow's on the other side of the field."

They walked over and within minutes were surrounded by a group of eager participants.

"Six pairs at a time," Russ directed loudly. "Everybody behind the starting line while Carly and I show the correct wheelbarrow racing position."

Suspicion flared within Carly when she watched Russ advance toward her with amusement on his face. His metal whistle bounced against the University of Tennessee tank shirt that did nothing to conceal well-developed pecs and broad shoulders. Denim cutoffs stretched over fascinating masculine bumps and ridges ending in the middle of muscular thighs dusted with curly auburn hair.

"You'll have to be the wheelbarrow since I'm bigger," Russ said. "You want to go ahead and get in push-up position?"

Carly was suddenly reluctant to have Russ Bradford staring down her spread legs. "That would be breaking the no-touch rules."

He frowned. "But we're responsible for showing these people the correct racing position."

She just bet they were. Carly wondered if he'd finagled these events for his purpose. Determined to cling to her sanity-saving rule, she said, "Perhaps you should get a volunteer."

Russ shook his head. "No. I'll be the wheelbarrow, and you carry my feet. You can do it. You're strong."

Carly put her hands on her biker shorts. "What about the no-touch rule?"

"That was about me touching you," Russ pointed out with a sly grin. "You can touch me anytime and any way you want, darlin'."

He looked at her with pure sensual invitation in

his eyes. Carly didn't know whether to slap him or kiss him. She rolled her eyes. "Okay, Bradford, hit the dirt."

Russ gave a long-suffering sigh, but got into push-up position.

Carly watched the way his wide shoulders tapered down to his waist and hard, taut derriere, and fought the scandalous urge to pinch him. She clenched her hands together.

"Do I have to wait all day?"

"No," she replied crossly. Then she picked up those tree trunks he called legs and strained and wobbled her way down the field.

An hour later, she found herself in the awkward position of trying to demonstrate a three-legged race while her partner kept his hands to himself. Every step forward seemed destined to throw them to the ground.

"This would be a hell of a lot easier if you'd let me put just one arm around you, Carly." Everything would be easier, Russ thought, if she'd let him keep his arms around her. She spent too much time alone thinking. If he could keep her in his house for one week with no interruptions, Russ felt sure he could persuade her to marry him. And it wouldn't be all sex, he thought. They would talk and eat and laugh and swim. He enjoyed her company. He enjoyed everything about her.

He cursed, tilting perilously toward the ground.

Carly grabbed his waist with both her hands. "Did anybody ever tell you that you weigh more than a bull?" She rubbed her forearm against the perspiration on her forehead. "You're entirely too large."

"Haven't you heard bigger is better?"

"Only from big people," she said, laughing.

Gasping for breath, they stopped. Russ noted the way her breasts nestled his side. Her soft, smooth thigh rubbed his rough, hard one. Her hand lay on his belly, torturing his imagination and libido. Her womanly scent filled his nostrils. Russ looked down at his empty, itchy, wanting hands and nearly wept with frustration. "Untie the ropes, Carly," he said through gritted teeth.

After the three-legged race, they took a break for lunch. Carly took one last bite of her barbecue sandwich and leaned back on her elbows. She lounged beneath a huge shady oak. A shadow passed over her, and she looked up. Carly gave a mock scowl. "You look nice and cool while I'm a sweaty mess. Go get a hot dog and spill some catsup on that fresh-looking blouse."

Sara sat down. "You don't look messy. You look like you've been having fun."

Carly offered her a piece of ice. "You always say the right thing. I don't understand why you're not married with a ton of kids."

Sara's face grew shuttered. "I lost my husband two years ago."

Immediately contrite, Carly sat up. "I'm sorry. That's horrible."

"Yes, it was." Sara looked into the distance. "We used to live in Chattanooga, but after Ron died, I guess I lost the desire to stay in the city. I need a slower pace where I don't have to fight the memories. To tell you the truth, this is the first time I've talked about it in a long time."

Carly studied her friend with the soft brown hair and winsome eyes. Though Sara was poised and efficient, Carly sensed a vulnerability about her. "Was it an accident?"

"Yes. The other car went out of control. Ron never knew what hit him. I'm thankful for that much."

Carly sighed and shook her head. "My mother died when I was four, then we lost Dad several years after that. It was tough, but my brothers practically smothered me trying to make up for the loss. You don't have any brothers or sisters. What about cousins?"

"None close to me. My parents' families were from Minnesota."

"How do you get over it, then?" Carly asked, wondering out loud. Her brothers had completely encompassed her with their love. She couldn't imagine facing that kind of grief alone.

"I'll never get over it," Sara said quietly. She looked at Carly. "I just take it one day at a time."

"Well, do you ever date or anything?"

A slow smile tugged at Sara's mouth. "No. Not even when my boss tries to push me and her brother together."

Carly grabbed Sara's hand. "Do you like him at all? Daniel's stubborn, but he's got a heart of gold. He's not bad looking. You'd be perfect for him. And maybe you wouldn't be so lonely."

Sara laughed out loud. Carly was happy to hear the rare sound after seeing such sadness on her friend's face.

"Daniel's handsome," Sara conceded. "He's also not interested in me."

Carly noticed Sara neglected to comment on whether or not she was interested in Daniel. "What makes you say that?"

Color tinged Sara's cheeks. "I overheard him tell one of your brothers what a shame it was that

Carly's assistant had such a . . . great body and such a stuffy personality."

Carly stared at Sara. "You're kidding." Then the situation struck her as funny and she began to laugh. Sara frowned at her, but Carly only laughed more. "I wonder what Daniel would do if he knew about those lingerie catalogs you have."

Sara smiled, but her eyes held a warning light. "He'll never know."

"Oh, I don't know. That kind of information has a way of leaking out."

"Carly."

"It would be for your own good. You're the kind of person who needs a family. I just want to help."

"You're one to talk about men. You've got Russ Bradford dangling on a long line."

Carly grimaced. "Russ Bradford doesn't dangle on anyone's line. He's got his own line, and he'll never settle down." The reality of that statement depressed her.

"Oh, I don't know," Sara said in a gentle mocking tone. "For a guy who'll never settle down, he sure seems to like children." She nodded at the group of children surrounding Russ.

Carly looked at him, his red hair glinting in the sun, his laughter inviting everyone within earshot to join in. He tossed a small boy in the air, then held the youngster like an airplane. They made buzzing sounds together until a little girl tugged on his leg. Russ gave the boy a hug, then set him down. He picked up the little girl and spun her around, sending her halo of blond hair flying.

If he ever found a woman he could love, Russ would make a wonderful father. Carly felt a tight squeezing in the region of her heart. An indescribable yearning swept over her. For a second, Carly wished she could be that woman, the one he'd love and never leave. The feeling shook her to the marrow of her bones.

"It's hopeless," she whispered more to herself than anybody.

"What?" Sara looked at her quizzically.

Carly shook her head, trying to clear it. "Nothing. Do me a favor and irritate Daniel a little bit. It'll be fun for you, and it might distract him. He owes you for that snotty statement he made about you."

Sara tilted her head thoughtfully. "Not that I would intentionally irritate your brother," she said after a long pause. "But what do you think would irritate him?"

"Oh, that's easy. Just tell him how much you admire his athletic ability, then mention how fortunate he is that he doesn't have to rely on his intellect for his success." Carly shared a knowing glance with Sara. "Daniel's the oldest, so he thinks he knows everything. It'll drive him crazy. Just make sure you smile when you say it."

"You're devious."

"I'm an angel compared to my brothers," she said, nodding at Russ as he waved her toward the stream. "I'll see you later. It's time for the tug-of-war."

She skipped over to him. "Who's on our team?"

"Butch Hollingsworth will lead. I'll bring up the rear."

Carly nodded. "I just wanted to know if I should prepare myself to get wet."

Russ rested one hand on his hip. "You wouldn't have to worry if you'd ditch the no-touch rule. I could keep you from going in."

"I'll risk the water," Carly said warily. "I'll eventually dry off."

"Are you saying my touch would leave a permanent mark?"

Carly's stomach took a dip. She tried to think of a witty response. When none came to mind, she walked ahead of him and took her position in the line of participants.

Russ came up behind her. She felt the warmth of his breath on her head. She shivered.

"You didn't answer my question," he said in a low voice close to her ear.

For the moment Carly was tired of the little game they played. She turned around and faced him. "Maybe your touch would leave a permanent mark on me, but it wouldn't affect you. I'm not interested in dealing with double standards anymore. My brothers have always had one set of rules for me and another for themselves."

"I'm not your brother."

"I know, but I guess I have enough self-respect not to want to be just another woman in your long line of conquests."

"What makes you think you could ever be just another woman?"

His face was serious. The lines etched around his eyes didn't crinkle in amusement. His jaw was set firmly. Her heart sped up. Foolish heart, she chided, to believe a man whose heart was better protected than the gold at Fort Knox. "This is crazy."

Russ opened his mouth to refute at the same time Butch Hollingsworth yelled for everyone to hold on. Carly turned around and tightly grasped the rope. She glanced at the other team and noticed Moose Gordon was their leader. Carly looked at the stream and winced. "You didn't tell me about Moose," she said over her shoulder. "Who else have they got?"

"The high school quarterback and Bertha Collins."

Great. Bertha was the local arm-wrestling champion. She beat most of the men. Carly took a deep breath and braced herself for an icy shock.

"You've still got time to break the no-touch rule. I'll pull you back. I won't let you go in."

He tempted her. Russ's arms won over an undignified plunge into the stream any day. Carly shook her head. "No thanks."

"I'll make you believe, Carly."

Carly swallowed hard. His simple statement brought a rush of excitement and fear. There was a loud cry, and the rope jerked. She heard Russ's growl of exertion and pulled with all her might.

She gained a foot of ground, then lost it within the blink of an eye. Butch cursed loudly. His wife fussed at him, and he cursed again. The team lost another foot. Carly felt increasingly impotent with each successive foot lost.

She kept her head down and dug in her heels. Still more ground was lost and she heard one splash followed by another. A howl of victory came from the other side. A few seconds later she watched the man in front of her tumble.

The rope jerked her off balance, and Carly plunged into the cold water. The shock against her heated skin took the breath from her lungs. Water seeped into her T-shirt and shorts. She sat up just as Russ made a slippery, forced landing with far more grace than she had. He only drenched his tennis shoes.

The spectators whistled and cheered loudly. Carly stumbled to her feet. She brushed back her hair and noticed that even it was wet. She looked up at Russ, coveting his relative dryness. "Show-off."

Russ plastered an innocent grin on his face and raised his palms. "No touch."

Carly drowned herself in work the following week. By Saturday, she was walking a ragged edge. The travel agents came, and she pulled out all the stops. The buffet was perfect. The waitstaff missed only a couple of notes and completely charmed the audience. Her brothers were handsome and cordial. Sara kept things in order, disappearing behind the scenes when necessary.

The travel agents left with promises to send their customers her way. Carly smiled until her cheeks hurt and retreated behind the bar. Her feet were killing her. It was these blasted heels, she knew. "Never again," she muttered to her poor, abused feet as she slipped off the shoes. Only Daniel, Sara, and the waitstaff remained. Russ's concerned face flashed in her mind. Her heartbeat picked up, and she found herself wishing she'd asked him to come. She cupped her head in her hands and seriously questioned her sanity.

Carly couldn't explain why she felt near to tears. Russ had been incredibly supportive, calling her everyday. He'd somehow managed to walk that fine line between concern and interference. He'd dropped in to see her twice and stuck to the no-touch rule. Strangely enough, his restraint left her with a sense of loss.

"Carly," Daniel said in a low voice.

She raised her head. "Yes."

"I'm not sure about Sara. She's completely taken over the waitstaff."

Her brother wore a look of bemused irritation. Carly smiled. "I asked her to take over. I'm beat. She's very efficient, isn't she?"

"Yeah," he said grudgingly.

"And she has this lovely calming effect on people. Don't you agree?"

He shifted and shoved a fist into his pocket. "Yeah."

Restraining the urge to chortle with glee, Carly studied her disgruntled brother. She gave a light laugh.

Daniel looked at her suspiciously. "What?"

"Oh, nothing," she said in a mild tone. "Sara seems so reserved. I was surprised when she gave me these catalogs full of sexy lingerie. She must keep all that wildness under wraps."

Daniel cleared his throat. "Lingerie?"

Carly nodded. "Everything. Lace, satin, silk. Red, black, sheer." She laughed again. "Men must sense her naughty streak. A few of those travel agents asked for her number."

"They did?" Daniel frowned.

Carly wasn't bluffing. She'd wondered if Sara disappeared to the galley partly due to the extra male attention paid her. The sense of glee she felt dissolved. "Yeah, but Sara's husband died in an accident a couple of years ago. She thinks she isn't ready for another man. It will take someone very special to draw her out."

Daniel looked thoughtful. "I wouldn't have guessed."

Carly's weariness suddenly overwhelmed her. After stepping into her shoes, she stood and actually felt the room spin. "I think I need to get into bed. Would you close up?"

"Sure. You want me to give you a ride?"

Carly shook her head. "No. It isn't far. Thanks for helping out tonight." She stretched to kiss him on the cheek. "See you later."

Trudging the short distance to her car, she planned a soothing bath and a glass of wine. Clouds shielded the stars and moon. She made a mental note to add another floodlight when she tripped over a large rock. The scent of impending rain hung in the air. She yawned and stretched, then bent to unlock her car.

She heard a scuffling sound on the gravel behind her and turned quickly. A blanket was thrown over her, and she was hoisted up in the air. For several paralyzing seconds a scream locked in her throat. She tried to take a deep breath and ended up sucking in the blanket.

She coughed and sputtered, and a garbled whimper finally came out of her mouth. Terror caused her heart to race as strong arms shoved her somewhere. Then she heard a door slam.

Immediately, instinctively, she began to struggle with the heavy blanket covering her. "Oh my God!" She was being kidnapped! The blanket seemed to go on forever. The more she struggled, the more tangled it became. Hysteria backed up in her throat when she heard another door open and close. The engine started, and the car moved forward.

Carly punched wildly, connecting with something hard. She heard a sharp oath and kept on hitting, even when the vehicle jerked to a stop. It was a man and he was saying something, but she was too frantic to listen. Her shoulders were grabbed.

"Carly!"

She paused. His voice sounded very familiar.

"Settle down, it's me, Russ. Nobody's going to hurt you."

She nearly passed out with relief. "Oh, thank God," she murmured weakly, still trying to catch her breath. Then she realized what he'd done, and a burst of anger hit her hard. "What do you think you're doing? You scared me to death. Get this blanket off me before I suffocate, you, you clod."

When he didn't respond, she shouted, "Now!"

Unmoved, Russ said, "You've got to promise that you'll sit there like a civilized human being and stop hitting me while I'm driving."

"Civilized? After you kidnapped me? Promise?" Her voice went up an octave. "The only thing I'll promise you, Russ Bradford, is certain death if you don't get this off me."

Russ sighed and snapped her seat belt together. "Guess you'll wear the blanket a little longer, then." He put the car into gear and drove forward.

Carly was incensed. She grew stuffy, and perspiration beaded her forehead. "Have you lost your mind? What are you doing?"

"I'm taking you home," he said calmly. "I'm fixing you a glass of wine you can drink while you take a bath in my Jacuzzi. Then I'm tucking you into my bed."

Carly's heart slammed against her ribs. "I can't sleep with you, Russ. What about the no-touch rule?"

"You won't be sleeping with me. I'll take a guest bed tonight."

A trickle of disappointment seeped in. She

brushed it away. "You touched me when you man-handled me into this truck," she accused.

"I touched a blanket," he corrected dryly. "If I was going to touch you, I sure as hell wouldn't allow any blankets between us."

"Russ, I'm burning up under this blanket. Please take it off so we can have a rational conversation."

"Will you act civilized?"

Carly ground her teeth together. "Yes."

He stopped the truck again, pulled the blanket from her, and tossed it behind the seat. He reached out to smooth her hair, then stopped midmotion. He gave a tight grin. "You okay?"

It was so good to see him again, to see the warmth in his eyes and hear his voice that she almost said yes. Her brain must have suffered from lack of oxygen when she was under that damned blanket, she thought, scowling. "No. I'm tired. My feet hurt. And I want to be in my own bed."

Russ's gaze fell over her from head to toe. He stared at her feet. "New shoes?"

Carly was glad the darkness hid her flushed face. Between the blanket and Russ's gaze, she was probably beet-red. "Yes. I'll never wear them again. I knew there was a reason I didn't wear high heels."

"I like them."

She curled her toes. "I don't."

"If your feet hurt that bad, I could always massage them for you," he offered graciously.

The image of his hands on her feet made her entire body tingle. She cleared her throat. "No. I want you to take me home."

"Can't do that." He looked at her face briefly and accelerated the truck.

"Russ, I don't like this. It's chauvinistic and macho. You're treating me like I'm some kind of concubine."

Russ chuckled. "Nah. If you were my concubine, you wouldn't have a job or your own apartment. You'd devote your entire life to pleasing me. As much as that idea intrigues me, I know you're not that kind of woman. Part of the reason you please me is because you're so independent."

Carly leaned back in the seat. She had to think about that. "It's chauvinistic. You're trying to make all my decisions for me."

"I am not. You can pick whatever wine you want. And I've got three different T-shirts you can choose from when you go to bed."

"I don't like this."

He turned into his driveway. "You will by Monday."

"Monday!" she said, aghast. She didn't know which bothered her more, two nights with Russ or a day away from work. "You know what I'm trying to do this summer. I can't take off an entire day."

"You don't have any cruises tomorrow. It's supposed to rain. It will be a perfect day for you to get some rest."

"It will be a perfect day to do bookkeeping."

Russ stopped the car. "The Jacuzzi's ready."

Carly sighed, feeling more weary than she'd ever felt in her life. "Russ, you shouldn't have done this."

He shook his head. "I had to do this. You're running yourself straight into the ground." He stopped for a moment, rubbing his mouth. "This is what friends do for each other. You need rest and a break from the books and your telephone. You need to be at a place where you don't feel like you need to cook and clean. You need somebody to take care of you." He held up a hand at her rebuttal. "Just for a little while. And I'm your friend, so I'm gonna do it. Then you can go back into battle."

Her arguments disintegrated. He made the prospect of staying at his home appealing, almost irresistible. She felt both vulnerable and safe. She watched him get out of the truck, circle it, then open her door. He stood there, waiting, one hand on the door, the other on a jean-clad hip, his eyes inscrutable.

Carly wavered. If she insisted, he'd take her back home. But she was emotionally and physically exhausted, and if she were honest with herself, she'd admit there was nowhere she'd rather be at this moment than with Russ Bradford. Carly shut off her mental processes. The implications of her thoughts were too disturbing, and she had a Jacuzzi bath waiting for her.

Six

If this was his idea of friendship, she'd hate to see an all-out seduction. The soft floral scent Russ had added to the bath teased her nostrils. Carly took another sip of the wine and reluctantly rose from the swirling water. He'd warned her not to fall asleep in the tub or he'd have to come pull her out. She giggled. Now how could he pull her out and stick to the no-touch rule? She felt giddy and languid. "You belong in bed," she told her hazy reflection sternly.

His bathroom was a retreat in white marble and jade. She squished her toes into the plush carpet. Surrounded by mirrors, Carly caught a glance of her peachy, damp skin and stared. For a moment, she imagined Russ seeing her this way. Her breasts felt full. Her nipples puckered. She licked her lips. The action was so provocative, she closed her eyes.

The room shifted and she laughed. The sound echoed lightly off the walls. She shouldn't have drunk the wine, she realized. Sighing, she toweled herself dry, then pulled on Russ's dark blue terrycloth robe as she stepped into his bedroom.

The decor combined subtle jade and gray to create a soothing effect. A long oak dresser with assorted male toiletries and pocket change lined one wall of the large room. A heavy oak armoire occupied another wall. The matching nightstand held a softly lit hurricane lamp and book. Curious, she looked at the author's name. Stephen King. Carly shook her head. Guaranteed nightmare material.

A P. Buckley Moss print of a young family settled in front of a roaring fire hung over his bed. The domesticity of the picture unsettled her. She heard a knock at the door and turned. Her heart beat faster. Pulling the robe around her more tightly, she said, "Come in."

Russ pushed open the door. "You okay?"

"Sure. Just looking around. I don't think I've seen this room since you remodeled."

Russ grinned. "I would have been glad to show you."

Carly turned away and finally looked at his bed. The bed he'd shared with several other women. Her insides twisted. "I think you've been busy showing others the last few years."

She felt him come up behind her. "Not here, Carly," he corrected quietly.

An inexplicable, yet boundless relief soared through her. "That's a lovely picture," she finally said to cover her seesaw emotions. "I didn't know you liked this artist."

Russ shifted, narrowing his eyes. "What did you expect?"

Carly shrugged. "I don't know. Nothing quite so, so familyish."

"Maybe a giant nude centerfold?"

"Well?" She raised an eyebrow.

His expression changed faster than a heartbeat. His gaze fell over her slowly, missing nothing. She felt the scorching path of his eyes and drew a quick breath.

"I don't need pictures." He cleared his husky throat and moved to the bed, gesturing toward the nightclothes he'd left for her.

Carly glanced at the array. "You lied. Those are not three T-shirts."

Russ gave a half-grin. "So sue me. Which one are you gonna wear? This one? It's the color of your eyes." The sight of his big, hard hands wrapped around the violet silk chemise sent a thundering sensation to her belly.

"What about this?" He held up a peach camisole. "Your skin is this color when you blush." He ran his rough fingers over the lace bodice.

Carly sank weakly to the bed. "Umm," she said around the giant lump in her throat. She snatched the clean, but well-worn University of Tennessee jersey from the bed. "I think this will do just fine."

Russ took one last lingering look at the delicate pieces and let them slide from his fingers. Then he turned to the jersey. "I wore this my last season at UT." He put his hands on his hips and shook his head, his eyes full of memories. "That shirt's had a gallon of my sweat washed out of it. When we beat Georgia, a running back sprayed me with champagne. My mom got that out, but there's a spot of blood that will be there forever." Russ sobered. "That was when my dad died. I slammed my hand into a locker."

Carly looked at him, feeling a powerful connection, an instant of deep mutual understanding. They'd both experienced grief, but they'd never truly shared it with each other. During that eye blink of time, the most private part of his mind met and merged with hers.

Then Russ seemed to remember he was breaking his own rule about keeping his deeper thoughts private. He gave an uneasy laugh and deliberately lightened his tone. "Bet you can't wait to put it on, now, between the blood and sweat."

She squeezed the faded yellow fabric and lifted it to her face. "Smells like fabric softener to me," she said in the same light vein, because the moment seemed incredibly intimate. She couldn't put a name to her feelings. They were too strong, too turbulent.

Russ looked with approval at her on his bed, cuddling his jersey against her neck and chest. He wished he were in that jersey. "I need to let you get some sleep," he said reluctantly. "Do you need anything?"

He watched her slowly shake her head. Her gaze remained on his as he backed toward the door. He'd better leave quickly. The sight of her on his bed was almost more than he could take. But Carly needed to hear herself make that move as much as he did, he knew.

Russ cleared his throat. "G'night. Let me know . . ." His voice trailed off.

". . . if I need anything." She nodded. "I will."

He closed the door and headed for the liquor cabinet.

"This is crazy," Carly whispered to herself after he left. The situation was impossible. If she had any sense, she'd put on her clothes and demand that Russ take her home. But she knew she had no intention of doing that. The next most sensible alternative was for her to pull on the old jersey, get into bed, turn out the light, and go to sleep.

Carly stripped off the robe and yanked the jersey over her head. Standing in the middle of the carpet, she felt completely surrounded. The room was his, the bed was his, the jersey was his. And she couldn't have felt less sleepy.

Rest! Who could rest? Russ Bradford was a pure shot of adrenaline to her system. Her body tingled and burned with unwanted restlessness. She ran her fingers through her hair in frustration. Maybe she should run around his house a few times. Maybe she could use his weight room. *Maybe she should take a cold shower.*

Carly groaned. She wasn't sure what had happened, but something inside her had shifted. Something had softened and yielded. The question of making love with Russ was no longer if. It was when. The desire she felt for him was as strong as the ocean's undertow, relentlessly pulling her farther and farther from safe shore. Carly closed her eyes. She only hoped she'd find a way back after the waves crashed.

The decision was made, she realized. She tried to take a deep breath but it seemed to catch in her throat. She touched her cheeks and found her skin burning as if she'd stayed out in the sun too long. Her stomach fluttered with anticipation. The only thing she could compare it to was the nervousness and excitement she'd felt before giving an oral book report in elementary school.

But she was no longer a little girl. She was a woman filled with need and desire for a man who was ready and willing to take her places she'd never been. She opened her eyes, and her gaze fell on the black high heels she'd discarded earlier. Before she lost her nerve, she stepped into them and started walking.

• • •

"Big mistake, bud," Russ muttered to himself. He stared at the second glass of whiskey and shook his head. The first one hadn't done a bit of good. This idea had been a huge mistake. The notion of Carly in his bed without him had his body screaming with outrage. He should be with her, touching her, kissing her, learning her pleasure and teaching her about his. Instead, he was sitting at his kitchen table trying to subdue a libido that would leave most teenage males in the dust.

He should be committed to the Beulah County mental facility. If things didn't change soon, he thought he probably would be.

He took another drink and hissed at the strong bitter taste. Then, hearing a sound, he turned his head and his heart just plain stopped.

The jersey ended midthigh, displaying her long silky legs to his gaze. On her feet were the heels. He blinked to make sure he wasn't seeing things. Yep, she had on the heels.

She clasped her hands tightly in front of her. She was chewing on her bottom lip, and her eyes were huge violet pools of uncertainty and desire.

"I, uh, I couldn't sleep," she said in a husky voice.

Russ couldn't help it. His gaze kept returning to her heels and the significance of her wearing them. He cleared his throat. "Neither could I."

She walked forward until she stood directly in front of him. Bending down, she touched the rim of his glass. "Y-Y-You don't n-need that." She jerked her hand to cover her mouth.

The slight stutter shook him. Russ watched her eyes fill with panic. She was embarrassed, he saw, and she looked ready to run. In one quick motion, he stood and reached for her. Then he paused, leaving his hands suspended a millimeter away from her skin. He gave a tight grin. "No touch."

Her eyelids fluttered downward, shielding her expression from him. Then lifting her hand ever so slowly, she raised it to his, matching palm to palm, thumb to thumb, and fingers to fingers. He watched in awe as she twined her soft, small hand with his and drew his hand to her mouth. An earthquake couldn't have affected him more than the sensation of her velvety lips against his skin. His heart pounded hard against his chest.

Unable to wait a second longer, he pulled her against him. "Are you sure?" he asked, praying she wouldn't change her mind.

"Completely, but I don't have any— I mean, I didn't bring anything—"

Russ hugged her and kissed her hair. "I'll take care of it." He pulled back and looked at her. "I'll take care of you."

"I haven't, you know, done—" She broke off and swallowed.

"I know. It'll be okay." He brushed her tousled hair back. "I promise." Then he hooked an arm beneath her legs and picked her up.

Caught off guard by the chivalrous gesture, she groped for her voice. "Is this part of the program?"

Russ shook his head slowly. "Everything's new tonight."

He lowered his head and kissed her. The room swam like a kaleidoscope and before Carly knew it they were in his bedroom and she was falling down on his big bed. She bounced against the plush quilt. A playful smile started inside her and spread to her lips.

Russ stood over her, unbuttoning his shirt and grinning back at her. He imprisoned one of her ankles firmly in his hand. Using only his index finger, he removed one high-heeled pump. He dangled it from his finger for a moment before he allowed it to drop to the floor.

Carly's heart was racing a mile a minute; still she couldn't prevent the giddy laugh that formed in her throat. "I thought you'd want me to keep them on."

Russ chuckled in return. It was a deep, naughty sound. "I figured you might get wild with passion and I'd be left with spike wounds in my back." He ran a finger down the naked sole of her foot.

She curled her toes. "Good thinking. I'd—" She sucked in a deep breath when he brought her foot to his lips and gently nibbled on her toe. All rational thought flew from her mind.

"Yes?" he prompted, as he discarded the other shoe and began to give the other foot equal attention.

Carly squirmed beneath his amused, wicked gaze. "Yes?" she repeated.

"You were saying?" His knee dug into the quilt as he leaned forward and skimmed his hard palms up her calves, past her knee to her lower thigh.

"I was?" Carly shook her head to clear it but the sensual fog hovered stubbornly.

Russ chuckled again, then bent to kiss her. All his kisses and touches over the last weeks, every teasing remark, and the times he'd said he wanted her, had kept her simmering for weeks. Simmering and unsatisfied. Hungry and eager, she welcomed his exploring mouth and tongue. Following his gentle sucking motion, she drew him deep into her mouth.

When he tried to gentle his caress, she ran her fingers through his hair and pulled him closer. He groaned and slanted his mouth against hers voraciously, as if he couldn't get enough of her. The playfulness that had tempered the passion vanished. Now there was only hot, aggressive need.

He pulled his mouth from hers and rested it against her shoulder, his breath coming unevenly. "Gotta slow down," he muttered. "Slow and easy." He seemed to be coaching himself.

Carly shook her head. "No," she whispered breathlessly. She couldn't joke anymore. The commotion inside her was riding the edge of pleasure and uncontrollable excitement. "I don't want slow and easy. I want you."

"Oh, Lord." He raised his head and looked into her eyes. "You don't know what you're saying."

With unerring feminine instinct, Carly knew halfmeasures wouldn't do. It was suddenly essential that she give herself to Russ as she'd never given herself before. Shameless and a little desperate, she reached up and slowly slid her tongue around his damp lips. "Then I guess you're gonna have to teach me."

Russ closed his eyes and tightened his grip on her shoulders. His big body shuddered.

Shifting slightly, Carly raised one knee so that she cradled him between her thighs. She felt his arousal and moved, once, experimentally, against him. He opened his eyes, and Carly's heart jolted at his expression. His face was taut, his brown eyes singed her with raw male hunger.

He thrust forward against her moist, silk-covered femininity, revealing the full force and implication of his intent. Her mouth went dry. Her body burned, steamy and feverish, from the inside out. Yet, he still seemed hesitant.

"Russ," she said around the lump in her throat, "why are we still dressed?" Then, with unsteady hands, Carly pushed the unbuttoned cotton shirt from his shoulders.

Russ pulled the jersey off her. As he kissed her, she pushed her fingers through the soft curly thatch of hair on his chest. She glided her hands over his corded muscles. She ran her fingernail over one tight male nipple and felt his gasp against her throat. Her panties disappeared next.

In a swift movement, he shucked his jeans and pushed her thighs farther apart to accommodate him. Carly braced herself for him, but he tantalized her with the intimate proximity, focusing his attention on her beaded, sensitive breasts.

With lips, tongue, and teeth, he teased her to distraction. Just when she thought he was finished, he sucked one engorged nipple deep into his mouth. At the same time, his hand traveled with lazy precision to her wet, aching core.

Carly choked out a cry.

But Russ wasn't through with her yet. While stroking the tiny nubbin of femininity, he slid one finger inside her. An unbearable tightness coiled within her. She arched off the bed, against his hand, against his chest.

"It's okay," he murmured.

But it wasn't. Beneath his hands and mouth, Carly hovered on the razor-sharp line of wrenching need. Tears came to her eyes. Her fingers clenched his broad shoulders in agitated movements. "Russ!"

Russ instantly stopped. "Am I hurting you?"

Carly could have wept. "No. Yes." The unsatisfied yearning threatened to burn her to cinders. "Don't leave me like this." She twisted restlessly against him.

"Oh, baby, I won't." He kissed her, then pulled back for a quick moment to protect her. "Put your legs around my waist," he murmured in her ear.

Carly complied, distantly feeling the fine sheen of perspiration on his skin, hearing the telltale roughness in his voice. His body was taut and hard against hers. He gently probed her entrance with his iron masculinity.

She looked at his face, a mask of sternly controlled need, and wanted to soothe and release him from his torment. She moved against him in a seeking, welcoming motion.

Russ gritted his teeth. "Don't move."

"Why?"

He cursed under his breath. "Just don't."

Carly didn't comply. She arched, drawing him in.

"Oh, God," he muttered. "I'm sorry." Then he thrust deeply within her.

Carly gasped. Her body stung, protesting the intimate invasion. They both lay there perfectly still. Russ's breath heaved.

After a long moment, he raised his head. "You okay?"

Carly didn't answer right away. Instead she wiggled experimentally.

Russ groaned, staring into deep violet eyes. Her lips were provocatively swollen from his kisses. Her breasts beaded against his chest. Her thighs wrapped around his waist like a silken chain. He couldn't remember wanting like this before. He wanted her body, her mind, her heart. Complete possession. Nothing else would do. If possible, he grew harder. The urge to mindlessly, repeatedly pump into her grew stronger with each passing second. "You okay?"

Carly wiggled again, the movement drawing him deeper into her and depleting his mental reserve. "I want—" she broke off when he rubbed his finger against her sensitized bud. "I–just want–more of you," she whispered brokenly.

Her womanly neediness stabbed his heart and shattered his control. Russ thrust against her. Her feminine walls grasped him while he watched with tender fascination as the motion of his persistent, caressing finger sent Carly into ecstasy.

She stiffened and her tiny internal tremors precipitated his own. Russ gave a hoarse growl of possession as he went over the edge into a bottomless well of release.

Moments later, Russ lay beside Carly, staring at her with fascination. He felt as though he'd just taken a ride on the world's fastest roller coaster and his body hummed with the aftershocks. His emotions were in an uproar. His mind spun in circles. It was no experienced painted lady responsible for his knocked-blindsided state, he realized in amazement. *It was little virgin girl-next-door Carly Pendleton.*

Unlike his other experiences with sex, Russ had no desire to leave his lover. He found he wanted to stroke her hair, to cuddle her, to share quiet conversation.

Following his inclination, he reached a hand to her tousled hair. "Carly," he whispered.

There was no response.

"Carly." He raised up to look at her. She faced the other direction. Her lips were sensuously puffy. Her open palm rested against her cheek in a gesture of vulnerability. He nudged her one last time to no avail. Her eyes remained stubbornly closed and her breathing relentlessly even. Russ's hellfire lover was sleeping like a babe.

The next morning Carly woke to the smell of bacon frying. Rain beat against the roof in a mesmerizing rhythm. It was a perfect day to stay in bed, she thought groggily. She snuggled deeper under the covers.

A male voice hummed the "Tennessee Waltz." Carly's eyes snapped open. She sprang upright in the bed. In Russ's bed, she realized with a strange sensation in the pit of her stomach. She peeked under the covers at her body, which bore several whisker burns in incriminating places, then she quickly got out of bed.

Carly hadn't expected sex with Russ to be so overwhelming, so passionate. She hadn't expected to beg him. Carly cringed at the memory. After knowing Russ all her life, she'd expected the fun and craziness, not such desperate need, and she wasn't exactly sure how she felt, let alone how to act this morning.

"Hey, Carly," Russ called from the hall.

She glanced down at her nude body and dashed into the bathroom. "I'll be out after my shower," she yelled, closing the door. Turning the water on full force, she resolved to present a more sophisticated, worldly attitude by the time she faced Russ.

Ten minutes later, she joined him at the table. "This looks great. I'm starving." She tightened the belt of the borrowed terry robe almost to the point of suffocation and smiled at him.

"Good," Russ said, and promptly planted a firm

kiss on her mouth. "You look great, too, in my kitchen, in my robe, in my bed."

His repeated use of "my" made her shift in her seat, but she decided to ignore it. Maybe it was just morning-after talk. "I like your robe. I may take it with me on Monday."

"Nah," Russ said, spooning eggs onto her plate. "If you took it to your apartment, you wouldn't have anything to use when you're here."

That was a huge assumption, in her opinion. "I was just joking," she said lightly.

Russ looked at her. "I wasn't."

Carly shrugged and bit into a piece of toast.

He lifted her chin with a finger and pinned her with his gaze. "You know, making love can change a relationship. People start thinking about permanency—"

Her throat closed just as she swallowed, and she broke into spasms of choking coughs. She gulped hot coffee and after scalding her tongue she shook her head. "Oh, no, Russ. You don't have to worry about that. I have no intention of getting into a permanent relationship with any man, just like you have no intention of entering a permanent relationship with a woman. I have no illusions about last night. You wanted me and I wanted you. That's as far as it went." She smiled, extraordinarily proud of herself. She sounded sensible and practical, almost worldly.

Russ stared as if she'd grown fangs and a beard.

She reached over and patted him on the shoulder, faltering at the memory of his bare body. Taking a deep breath, she said, "I don't want you to feel an unnecessary responsibility for me just because last night was my, uh . . ."

"First time," he finished for her. "It sounds like you

think this is a one-night stand, Carly. I thought I made it clear that one time wouldn't be enough for either of us. After last night, I'd think you'd realize that too."

"Not a one-night stand," she corrected quickly. "I was thinking more in terms of a, uh, an affair." This had sounded so much better in the shower. "That way, you won't have to worry about me expecting marriage, and I'll be able to keep my independence. You were so smart to think of this arrangement."

She was blaming *him* for this idea! Russ cracked his knuckles underneath the table, then brought a hand to the back of his neck and rubbed. If her brothers didn't wring her neck, maybe he'd do it himself. He'd been sure their sweet intimacy would bring her desire for a committed relationship to the surface. Once again, he'd miscalculated. Russ sighed. "Better eat your eggs before they get cold."

Throughout the meal, Carly attempted small talk, but Russ appeared distracted. Her confidence waned with each conversational dud until she became quiet and finished in silence. They cleared the dishes from the table, and she wondered miserably what her morning-after faux pas had been. Well, there was no sense in remaining in such an uncomfortable situation especially if Russ didn't want her here. "I'd appreciate it if you'd give me a ride home. This would be a good time to take care of some of my bookkeeping."

"Nah." He turned on the dishwasher. "It's Sunday and it's raining."

Carly frowned. "What does that have to do with anything?"

Russ pulled on the lapels of the robe she wore until

she stood an inch away from him. Then he put his mouth against her ear.

Carly's stomach knotted.

"There's only one acceptable activity for lovers on a rainy Sunday afternoon, Carly." He ran a string of kisses down her neck, approving her faint shiver. It had taken the entire meal for him to formulate his plan. If Carly wanted an affair, then that was exactly what she would get. Russ planned to give her the affair of her life, the affair to last her life. The affair that would lead to a September wedding. He loosened the belt of the terry robe, pushed it from her shoulders, and felt heat flood his veins at her naked beauty.

"You want an affair, lady?" Russ kissed her, then placed her hands on the buttons of his shirt. "It's a tough job, but somebody's got to do it."

Carly hesitated, then undid his buttons. Slowly, her lips lifted in a smile that turned sultry. "Russ, if you find the prospect that unpalatable, I wouldn't want you to put yourself out."

Russ chuckled. "You're too sassy for your own good."

"Oh, yeah?"

"Yeah." He gave her fanny a quick smack and smiled at her shriek as he hauled her over his shoulder in a fireman's hold.

"It's not afternoon, you big lug," she told him as he walked unmistakably toward the master bedroom.

"I like to get an early start. We can just practice."

"You're quiet," Russ said as he turned the corner into her apartment's parking lot. "What are you thinking about?"

Carly glanced at Russ. He wore a casual shirt and jeans. His jaw was shadowed with surprisingly attractive stubble. He hadn't shaved, instead saying he preferred to spend the time with her.

He was her lover now, and she would never be able to look at him in the same way. He'd been tender, funny, and sexy. She'd had a wonderful weekend. But there was something beneath his manner that made her uneasy. He was demonstrative when they made love, and with the exception of that one moment when he'd talked about his father, he kept conversation light and breezy. He was keeping his heart under wraps, she realized, just as she'd always known he would. She stirred restlessly, struggling with an odd twinge of disappointment.

"Work," she finally replied. That's what she *should* be thinking about.

"Work? Is that why you're wearing that lost-puppy-dog face?" He pulled the truck to a stop and turned off the engine.

"Russ, this may shock you, but I don't like being compared to a lost puppy dog."

"Testy, too, huh?"

His accuracy irritated her. "I'm not testy."

Ignoring her prickliness, he hauled her into his lap.

She struggled. "I'm being squashed."

Russ shifted. "I'm feeling testy too. You didn't wear either one of those slinky nighties the whole time you were at my house."

She pursed her lips against the amusement bubbling within her. He sounded like a little boy denied his favorite ride at the fair. "You didn't give me a chance."

"I didn't?" He gave a heavy, long-suffering sigh. "I

guess you'll just have to wear them next time. How about tonight?"

Carly's laugh escaped. "No. I've got a ton of work."

Russ ignored her. "I've got an even better idea. Why don't I move your things over to my house today and you can just go ahead and move in?"

Sheer terror clogged her throat. "No!" she squeaked out.

Russ's eyes narrowed. His demeanor became serious. "Why not?"

Carly laughed nervously, filling the awkward silence. She didn't want to offend him, but the idea of moving in with Russ Bradford reeked of commitment, and the notion of committing herself to a man she was unsure of seemed stupid. She gave him a quick kiss and scrambled to the other seat. "You're too distracting. That's why not." She pushed open the car door and got out.

Russ met her on the sidewalk and captured her hand in his. "Okay, I'll put a hold on the moving truck. When can I see you again? Tuesday night?"

Carly shook her head.

"Wednesday?"

She shook her head again slowly.

"Thursday?"

Carly grimaced when she thought of her schedule.

"You know, if I were lacking in self-confidence, you'd be doing severe damage to my ego."

"Yes, but you don't lack self-confidence," she pointed out.

"I'd hate to have to resort to kidnapping again."

"Thursday night," Carly said.

Seven

"You want what?" Troy and Daniel asked at the same time.

Russ took a long swallow of beer and prepared himself for yet another battle for the sake of Carly Pendleton's hand. "I want to buy your shares in *Matilda's Dream.*"

Troy's face wrinkled in confusion. "Why? I thought you were keeping busy with your catfish operation."

Garth shifted in his seat. "He's gonna marry Carly."

"Who?" Daniel demanded.

Russ sighed. He'd hoped the steak dinner and beer would soften them up, make them a little more reasonable. He waved to the waitress and pointed to his bottle. It looked as though he was in for a long night. Then in a firm voice, he announced, "I plan to marry Carly this fall."

Troy stared, then smashed his hand against the table and burst out laughing. Jarod joined in uncertainly. Garth shook his head, and Daniel frowned.

"He's not kidding, Troy," Garth said. "He's had this planned since the beginning of the summer."

Troy's laughter abruptly ceased. He looked at Russ in disbelief. "Not you. Everybody knows you'll never settle down. Hell, even the women know it."

That statement touched a sore spot in Russ. It was the same thing Carly would say. Russ narrowed his eyes. "Well, then everybody's wrong. Carly and I are spending a lot of time together, and if everything goes according to plan, we'll be married in September."

The waitress delivered another round of beers to the silent group. Jarod cleared his throat. "When did you decide this?"

"I've been thinking about it for about two years, but Carly wasn't ready. I thought I'd give her some space."

"And you think she's ready now?" Daniel shook his head. "How does she feel about it?"

She's not ready, Russ thought, but he planned to change that. "I'm doing everything I can to persuade her."

Troy lifted an eyebrow. "Everything?"

Russ felt the immediate surge of tension in the air and leaned back from the table. "What's between Carly and me will stay between Carly and me. You can rest assured that she has feelings for me and I'll never hurt her."

"What does this have to do with *Matilda's Dream*?"

Russ smiled grimly at Jarod's question. "Carly's got some plans that need to be nipped in the bud. I can't tell you what they are. I promised her I wouldn't. You're just gonna have to trust me on this one."

Troy scowled. "Trust you with Carly? Do you think we're idiots?"

Russ ground his teeth together, reminding himself that Troy had always possessed a tendency to speak without thinking. "You have every reason to trust me. You've all known me forever. You know I'm a man of my word."

"You're also a man who's had a string of women a mile long," Troy retorted. "How do we know Carly's any different?"

Russ rolled his eyes heavenward. "Do you really think I'd do this for anybody else? Hell, by buying your shares, I'm tying up money I wanted to invest in a co-op."

Daniel looked at Troy. "He's got a point."

"Yeah, but why Carly?"

Russ felt the tug and pull of a hundred emotions warring inside him. He thought of Carly's honest, generous nature. He thought of her womanly allure. He couldn't explain it to himself, so how could he possibly explain it to her brothers? "We suit," he finally said. "I'm committed to her, but she's pushing this independence thing. If I don't rein her in now, who knows what kind of guy she'll end up with? At least, I'm a known quantity. You could do a lot worse."

Russ felt as though he were trying to sell a horse. Should he show his teeth and give a medical release next?

"She has been acting independent lately. Maybe this would be best." Jarod looked at Russ in a new appraising way. "You're gonna have to cut out all your carousing."

Russ rubbed his mouth to hide his grin as he remembered how their darling little sister had worn him out in bed. He cleared his throat. "There won't be any more carousing," he said in a mild voice. Hell, he wouldn't have the energy or the inclination for it. "So, what'll it be? Will you sell me your shares or not?"

Garth spoke first. "You've got mine."

Daniel nodded. "Mine too."

Garth fiddled with his bottle for a few moments. "Okay."

Troy jutted out his chin. "Well, I don't know. Why are you keeping all these secrets? Why won't you tell us why you want to buy us out?"

Russ made a noise of exasperation. "Troy, I think you'd argue what shape the earth is. I told you why I can't tell you. I promised Carly, and I don't break my promises. But if you want to take your chances"— Russ shrugged his shoulders—"it's your choice. I'd hate to see her end up like Mary Weaver."

Troy paled. "Mary Weaver took off to Tanzania with that guy who walked around chanting all the time." He took a gulp of beer and stared at Russ as if for the first time. "So I've got to pick between you and Tanzania?"

"I didn't say that," Russ said, stifling his laughter. "You've got to pick between the known and the unknown."

Troy sighed and gave a disgruntled snort. "I guess it'll have to be you, then."

Russ smiled thinly. "Glad I have your full support. What about Ethan, Nathan, and Brick?"

"No problem," Daniel said. "They'll go with the majority."

"Good." Russ looked at the varied expressions on the faces of his future brothers-in-law. Despite Troy's underwhelming agreement, a feeling of satisfaction edged in at the battle he'd just won. It was a step closer, another barrier removed. Russ's smile grew, unfurling from the excitement inside him. For once, everything was going according to plan.

Late Thursday afternoon, Carly returned to the office after making an extended sales call to National Electronics. She smiled at Sara as she swept through the door. "I've got a banquet for NE booked next month."

"Great!"

Carly kicked off her shoes. "The director said he'll give us a try and if they like us, we can expect four bookings a year." She thought about the bank vice president she'd talk to last week and wondered if this news would help her case. "Any messages?"

Sara handed Carly a stack of pink message slips. "Several."

The first one was from Daniel. *Russ will do just fine.* Carly wrinkled her brow. What did that mean? The next one from Garth said *Russ is a good, solid guy.* Carly frowned. The one from Troy was so ridiculous she read it out loud. "You could do worse than Russ." She looked at Sara. "What is going on?"

"It looks like they're putting their seal of approval on Russ." Sara laughed. "I didn't write it down, but Troy also said, 'At least Russ doesn't chant.' Two of the others are from Russ. He said he'd pick you up around five for dinner."

"But why?" Carly frowned in confusion. "Why would they give their approval?"

Sara shook her head. "I don't know, but three of the other messages are from travel agents. If you're going to call them today, you'd probably better go ahead."

Carly nodded, heading for her office.

"Maybe Russ knows something about it. You can ask him when you see him tonight," Sara called after her.

Carly walked behind her desk and slowly sat down. *Maybe Russ knows something about it.* She tensed, as she did every time she thought of him.

Carly didn't like the feelings she was experiencing. Whenever the phone rang, she wanted it to be him, yet she had to fight to get back on an even keel after hearing his voice. When he laughed, a knee-weakening thrill ran through her. Her skin heated when he told her he missed her. It was ridiculous, she scolded herself. But it didn't stop. She'd become a lump of emotional, feminine mush.

Scowling, she crumpled the messages from her brothers and Russ into a ball and tossed them at the wastebasket. This must stop, she told herself. Just last night, she'd lain awake wondering what Russ's true feelings for her were. Sure, she was special to him. But how special?

Carly closed her eyes, feeling the beginnings of a headache. Maybe she wasn't cut out for affairs, she thought. Maybe they should go back to being friends. Fat chance, her conscience chided.

Slamming the door on her thoughts, she forced her eyes open, read the travel agent's message and, with excessive vigor, punched out his number.

A few minutes later, Russ appeared at her doorway. Her chest tightened, but she kept her cool and waved him in. "Yes, Mr. Emerson, we're delighted to be included in your tour. With the number of people you're talking about, we can arrange a special rate.

I'll get the information in the mail to you tomorrow." Carly paused to let the agent say his good-bye. "Thank you again."

She hung up the phone and lifted her head to greet Russ, but his kiss preempted her words. His hand slid behind her neck while his warm mouth caressed hers in a teasing, intimate way. Her nerve endings hummed and her mind went blank.

He pulled away and looked down at her. "Hi. I've missed you."

Her heart swelled. "I, uh, hi." She cleared her throat. Of their own accord, her eyes drank in the sight of him. He wore a blue short-sleeve pullover and black cotton pants. The open shirt revealed his curly chest hair. Hair she'd run her fingers through and buried her face in, Carly remembered.

Russ grinned. "Where do you want to eat? We can go into Chilham for seafood if you want to."

Carly shook her head. "No. I'm tired and hungry. I had a business lunch, and I was too nervous to eat. The Davy Crockett Diner will be fine with me."

He held out his hand to her. "Business lunch. Was it successful?"

Carly hesitated, then accepted his hand. "Yes, but my prospects for a loan are still shaky." She caught sight of the discarded ball of pink message slips on the floor and stiffened slightly. "There's something I need to talk to you about."

Russ pulled her closer and studied her. "Go ahead."

Uncomfortable under his scrutiny, she shook her head and pulled him toward the door. "After dinner. I can't think on an empty stomach."

Russ allowed her to lead him to the car although he had a disquieting premonition. He'd noticed how she avoided his eyes. She'd responded to his kiss, but immediately withdrew. And damn if she hadn't almost refused his hand. Then she'd said that business about how she couldn't think on an empty stomach. Lord help him. If she started thinking, he was a dead man.

After Carly picked at her Salisbury steak and refused dessert, Russ became more suspicious. His own gut was starting to twist. "Coffee. No dessert," he told the waitress as she cleared the table. "I'm waiting, Carly."

Carly took a breath and folded her hands in her lap. She deliberately kept her voice casual. "Have you seen my brothers, lately?"

Russ shrugged. "I see them all the time. We went out to dinner the other night."

She nodded. "What do you talk about when you get together?"

He shrugged again. "Anything. Farming, the economy." He grinned. "The Braves."

"Women?"

"Sometimes." His smile fell. "Why?"

"I got some messages from them today, and I wondered if you'd told them about this weekend." She flashed a searching look at him, then back to the Formica table and waited out a long silence.

Russ cleared his throat. "What happened this weekend was private. I wouldn't share that with anybody."

Carly felt an instant easing within her. "It must have been someone else. You're not the type to kiss and tell."

Russ shifted. "I didn't tell them about this weekend, but I did tell them about my intentions toward you."

"Intentions?" She leaned forward. "You told them we're having an affair?" she whispered tersely. Carly wondered how he'd escaped alive.

Russ frowned. "No. I didn't say anything about an affair. I said we were . . . serious."

Carly searched Russ's face for signs of insanity. "Have you lost your mind? They'll expect you to marry me now." She sighed and looked away, shaking her head.

"Would that be so bad?"

His words hit her like a cyclone, stirring her senses and emotions into a flurry of confusion. The room swam. She put her hand to her chest to collect herself and stared at Russ. "It wouldn't be bad. It would be horrible! Especially since we have no intention of getting married."

Russ met her gaze dead on. "Speak for yourself."

Her eyes widened. A heart attack was next, she was sure of it. He couldn't stun her anymore. "I thought," she said shakily, "we agreed to an affair."

Russ nodded, and Carly felt a measure of relief.

"A permanent affair," he said. "That's what marriage is."

She blinked. This couldn't be happening, she thought. It was crazy. Carly bent her head and brought her hand to her forehead. "This doesn't make sense," she whispered to herself.

"It makes perfect sense," Russ said in a matter-of-fact voice. "We're compatible. We were both raised on farms, so we understand each other's background. We respect each other."

Carly ignored the dance going on in her stomach and tried to focus on his words. She still couldn't comprehend Russ. "But this is so sudden and I thought—"

"—you thought I was just fooling around with you." Russ shook his head. "I hadn't intended to tell you this soon, but I've been thinking about marrying you for a long time."

Troubled, Carly shook her head. "But what about the Ladies Auxiliary? What about how you wanted me to help you because I wouldn't misunderstand your—" Carly broke off, a sliver of light dawning in her dark muddled mind. She looked at Russ accusingly. "It was a trick."

Russ held up a hand. "Now, don't jump to conclusions. You've been so wrapped up in that riverboat of yours, I had to use extreme measures to get your attention."

Her indignation built. "So you lied."

Russ winced. "That's a harsh way of putting it."

Her hands turned to ice, her sense of betrayal was so great. "What else did you lie about? Did you tell my brothers I wanted to buy them out? Did you lie about wanting me in bed?"

Russ reached out and tightly clasped her hand. "That wasn't fair. If you need me to prove my desire for you, I can do it anytime, any place. I could show you right now on this table if the audience wouldn't bother you."

Carly's breaths came quickly, harshly. She jerked her hand away. She felt toyed with, manipulated, and painfully vulnerable. At that moment, she couldn't say who deserved her fury more—Russ for manipulating her or herself for letting him. On top of her other doubts, this was too much. She stood. "I'm going home."

He reached for her, but she slid out of reach. "You don't have a car, and I don't want you leaving all upset."

"I don't have much choice about leaving upset, Russ, but I'm not leaving with you." She started walking toward the door without a backward glance.

Russ stared after her and threw some bills on the table. In a few quick strides, he caught up with her, stepped around her, and opened the door. She paused, but walked through.

"Carly, we can't just leave it like this. There's too much unfinished business. Let me take you home."

Carly absently nodded at an acquaintance and kept moving. "As far as I'm concerned, our business is very finished."

Russ's heart sank. He'd had no idea she'd get so upset. "Do you mean that?" He clamped a hand over her shoulder and turned her around. He stared into eyes that chilled him with their disappointment. "You really don't want me anymore?"

"It seems like what I want hasn't mattered all that much." Her body was tense as a bow, but her eyes looked moist.

Russ tenderly touched her cheek. "It matters to me," he assured her. "What do you want, Carly?"

"I want to go home," she whispered.

Russ wanted to take her anywhere except her apartment. Because once there, she'd say good night and she'd have the whole night to let her anger and hurt build. He'd be back at square one, if he was lucky. He wanted to take her to his house and work everything out. But that unsteady whisper felled him sure as a well-placed ax fells an oak. With a heavy sigh and a heavier heart, he ushered her to his car.

Carly stripped off her clothes, pulled on a night-shirt, and crawled onto her bed, holding the pillow in her arms. The white-hot anger was still inside, heating her, making her acutely aware and acutely awake. She wouldn't sleep tonight, she knew.

Naive little girls shouldn't play with fire. Russ Bradford was fire and she felt charred. She pressed her lips together and looked down at her pink sheets. Holding on to her anger, she realized she had no one to blame but herself. Hurt surfaced in spurts, and she wanted to avoid it. If she stayed angry, she wouldn't have to face the sharp, stunning pain. Her face was tight with the effort to hold back tears.

In spite of the fact that Russ couldn't be trusted with a woman's heart, she'd trusted him. Because of their long friendship she'd thought they shared a mutual respect.

Carly scowled. For all his teasing and flirting, some stupid secret part of her had begun to believe him. With stinging accuracy, she recalled his practical marriage plans. He'd mentioned nothing of love or need.

Tears began to blur her vision. She wiped her cheeks with her hands. He'd tricked her into an affair, then he'd listed his emotionless reasons for wanting to marry her the same way he'd list the reasons why one catfish grain was better than another.

Carly threw the pillow across the room. She wouldn't give her heart to a man she couldn't reach. She'd done it for years with her father. How many times had she tried to win her father's approval and been rewarded with an absent pat on the head? She stared at the ceiling and remembered the pictures she'd drawn for him in elementary school, the good grades. When that hadn't worked, she'd turned into a tomboy so she could work by his side. But her father hadn't allowed it, saying he had sons for that. How many times had she cried herself to sleep?

Intellectually, Carly knew her father had been caught in his own pain from the loss of her mother. She knew that in his way, he'd done his best. He'd found a new wife willing to care for eight children. Unfortunately that new wife had resented the fact that Carly bore a startling resemblance to her mother. Eunice couldn't be faulted for stepping in as caretaker, but Carly was sure Eunice had wanted more from her father too. Perhaps in another situation, that could have drawn Eunice and Carly together. In this case, it drove them apart. Whatever her reasons, Eunice had always kept Carly at arm's length. And because of his own silent grief, her father had done the same.

Carly remembered wanting him to cuddle her in his arms. She remembered making a wish on her ninth birthday that her father would say he loved her. She waited year after year. He'd died when she was thirteen and Carly had still been waiting. She'd learned so well the cruel reality that some things were hopeless.

Falling back on the bed, she felt a sob build and grow in her chest until her willfullness could no longer hold it back. Warm salty tears streaked down her cheeks. Turning on her side, she wept again until she fell asleep.

The next morning was worse. Her face was a mess of tight, splotchy skin. She had a crick in her neck, and her head felt as though Custer's Last Stand was being fought inside it. Her eyes were a festive red, white, and purple.

Carly grimaced at her reflection in the mirror and took extra time with makeup. She wore heavier foundation, put drops in her eyes, and took two aspirin. But aspirin couldn't do a thing for her heart.

By four o'clock, she was ready for a good stiff drink. Carly stared at the phone in her office.

Sara stood in the doorway, eyeing Carly with a worried expression on her face. "Russ called again. He said if you didn't take his next call he'd come see you personally."

Carly sighed. "Okay, put him through next time."

Sara walked in and sat in the chair across from Carly. "You never told me what the bank vice president said."

Carly gave a brittle smile. "He said he was sorry, but with the current condition of the economy they were forced to be conservative with their business loans."

"I'm sorry."

"It's been that kind of day. I got a cancellation for a banquet too."

"What about Russ?" Sara asked quietly.

Carly took a deep breath. Her chest felt tight and achy. She shook her head. "That's not working out."

"Carly, I know you're my employer, but I think of you as a friend."

"That's because you *are* my friend."

Sara pushed her hair behind her shoulder. "Well, you look miserable. Shouldn't you talk to him?"

"No," she said quickly. "He did something that—" She bit her lip. "Well, let's just say I feel really stupid."

The phone rang and Carly just looked at it.

"It's probably Russ," Sara said.

"Yeah."

"You want me to take it?"

"Yeah, but I'll do it." She braced herself, then picked up the receiver. *"Matilda's Dream."*

There was a long pause. "Carly? Is that you?" Russ asked in a rough voice.

She looked at Sara and nodded. Sara slipped from the room. "Yes, it's me."

"You haven't taken my calls," he said.

"I've been busy." She twisted the cord. "It's been a rough day."

Russ gave an audible sigh. "No kidding. I haven't been able to do anything right today. We need to talk."

Carly vigorously shook her head, forgetting to speak.

"Carly, we need to talk."

She heard the need in his voice. God, was she fooling herself again? "Not now," she said over the lump in her throat. Her voice fell to a whisper. "I can't talk to you now."

"But when?" he asked, frustration edging in.

"I don't know. I just can't talk to you now." She had to get off the phone before she broke down. She was appalled at the way her eyes filled with tears. "I've gotta go. Bye, Russ." She hung up the phone to the sound of him calling her name.

Sara immediately stepped through the door again with a box of tissues. "I thought you might need these."

Carly took one and dabbed her eyes. Then she blew her nose. "This is ridiculous. I've got to stop."

"Is there anything I can do?"

"No. I wish I had an on-off switch in my brain. I'd turn it off." Carly moaned and pounded the desk with her fist. "If I were Jarod or Daniel, I'd probably head over to that wild saloon in Chilham, flirt a little, drink a lot, and have Garth drive me home."

"Is that one of those strip joints?"

"Nah. It's just a big, honky tonk bar."

Sara tilted her head thoughtfully. "Is it a safe place?"

Carly shrugged. "I guess so."

"Then I think we should go."

Carly did a double take. "You're kidding."

Sara squared her shoulders with what Carly thought looked like defiance. "I'm not. You need to let off a little steam tonight. This sounds like just the place to do it."

Carly tried to imagine serious Sara in such a setting and couldn't help but smile. "My brothers would kill me. I remember once back in college when they threatened to lock me up for a week if they ever saw me there."

"They can't lock you up now."

That gave Carly pause. She'd been forced to accept her brothers' rules for so long that she complied without thinking. She'd been saying she wanted her independence. Maybe it was time to put her money where her mouth was. "You're on. Let's go change clothes. Can you pick me up in an hour?"

Sara and Carly stood at the same time. A slow smile grew on both their faces. "We're probably going to hate this," Carly pointed out.

Sara nodded. "Yes, but we can think of it as an educational experience."

Two hours later, Carly's head was numb from the pounding music of the live band. "It's so loud, I can't think," she yelled at Sara.

Sara smiled. "That's the idea."

A man came to stand in front of her and grinned. He pushed back his cowboy hat. "You need to dance," he said in a deep drawl.

Carly was about to decline as she had several other times, when Sara stunned her by speaking up. "She does. She just needs a little encouragement."

Carly cut her eyes at Sara. "I—" Before she could finish, he took her hand and pulled her to her feet.

"Your feet were growing roots into the floor." He made a disapproving clicking noise. "It would have been hell for the owners to dig you out by the end of the night."

A reluctant smile tugged at her mouth. His eyes were a friendly blue, and she had to admit his approach was original. "All right. But if you call me a filly, I'll stomp on your feet."

He laughed good-naturedly and swung her into a fast two-step. Before long, she found herself in another man's arms, then another, and another. The room became a kaleidoscope of different music and different men. She lost track of how many songs had passed, but one man kept showing up. His name was Jim, and he held her a little too close and he complimented her effusively while he tried to talk her into going back to her apartment.

Carly shook her head. "No. I'm just out for fun tonight. Nothing heavy."

"I'm out for fun tonight too."

"Not that kind of fun," she said firmly, thinking that his eyes were the same caramel color as Russ's.

"You don't know till you try," he pointed out.

Carly thought of how tied up in knots she'd been over Russ. "I don't want to try tonight." She stepped back, putting some space between them. She hoped the song would be over soon. This was getting sticky.

Jim stepped forward, eliminating the space. "There must be something I can do to persuade you."

Growing increasingly uncomfortable, Carly backed away and looked around the smoke-laden room. "I really don't—" She broke off when she spied two familiar figures in the back of the room.

She stiffened and felt her stomach fall to her feet. The instinct of twenty-three years slammed into her. Daniel and Russ stood at the door, their gazes planted on her and her dance partner. Daniel was scowling. Russ looked ready for blood.

She turned back to Jim, wincing at his seductive expression. She shook her head, "Jim, I really—"

Jim's middle name must have been persistence. At that moment, he dipped his head and planted a firm kiss on her mouth.

Carly forcefully pushed him back. "You're going to regret that."

Jim just smiled. "I couldn't regret it."

"You will when all your teeth are gone." Carly took a quick glance over her shoulder. "You see those two guys walking toward us?"

"Yeah."

"The dark one will probably kill me," she said, wishing she were anywhere but here. Siberia sounded good.

Jim's smile wavered. "Don't worry. I'll talk to him."

Carly shook her head and sighed. "No. The red-haired one will probably kill you."

Eight

Within seconds, Russ and Daniel were bearing down on her. Jim must have possessed strong survival instincts, because he disappeared. Carly fought the urge to run at the same time she looked for the emergency exits. She had about two eye blinks to get her stuff together. Since she didn't have the emotional stamina for a fight, she opted for a breezy hello and good-bye.

"Fancy meeting you two here," she said with a painfully bright smile.

Daniel glared. "What are you doing here?"

Russ was busy surveying the crowd for her elusive suitor.

Carly's throat clenched at the image filling her mind of broken chairs, broken glass, and broken body parts. "I, uh, I'm here with Sara."

"Sara!" Daniel's frown darkened.

Carly covertly watched the expression in Russ's eyes and vowed to leave as soon as possible. His usually warm, caramel eyes were cold as January.

She shivered despite the heat in the room. "There's Sara," she said, edging away. "She's waving to me now. Guess it's time to go. See you guys later." She turned and walked swiftly toward the table.

Her deep breath of relief was premature. A strong, callused hand enclosed her arm, stopping her midstride. A powerful sense of dread began in her stomach and spread to her toes. Carly didn't want to look at Russ's face right now. She felt dangerously close to a mammoth explosion of anger or tears, and Carly knew either would bring regret. "Yes?" she said without turning to face him.

"You're riding home with me. We're way overdue for a talk."

"That sounds like an order. I don't respond well to orders."

His staggered sigh ruffled her hair. Even without seeing his face, she could feel the frustration rolling off of him.

"Will you ride with me?"

"Thank you very much, but I already have a ride with Sara." Carly tried to skip away, but she might as well have been padlocked to him.

"Sara's taking Daniel home. You can ride with me."

Her anger pricked at his calm, implacable tone. Carly spun away from him. "I don't want to."

He turned her around and lowered his head. Her heart stopped. Was he going to kiss her?

"Tough," he muttered an inch from her mouth, then nudged her toward the door.

Although Carly wanted to ask Russ how he'd known she'd gone to the bar, she didn't speak one word on the drive home. She considered slamming her apartment door in his face, but Russ was right on her heels. The excruciating silence continued while she flicked on a light and kicked off her shoes.

She'd rather eat worms than have this discussion. It was going to be awkward. She'd probably get teary and emotional while Russ remained logical and remote. There'd be no satisfactory conclusion. Russ would leave confused, with his emotions intact, and she'd probably cry herself to sleep.

"It's late," she began hopefully. "Maybe another time would be—"

Russ shook his head before she finished the sentence, and Carly sighed in defeat. She started to sit down on the sofa, then thought better of it and took a chair. A one-person chair instead of a two-person sofa where people talked and touched and made love. Carly bit her lip.

Russ remained standing. "Something went wrong the last time we saw each other. Is it your brothers?"

She took a deep breath and shook her head. "No."

He stepped closer. *"Matilda's Dream?"*

The smell of his after-shave teased her memory. "Not really."

"Why won't you look at me?" he demanded.

Carly snapped her head up and finally met his gaze of displeasure. Her anger kicked in. She stood. "I told you I didn't want to talk."

"Why?" he asked stonily.

"I can't explain it, and even if I could, you'd never understand."

"Give it a try."

"Why?"

"'Cause I'm not leaving till you do."

Carly glared at him. "Okay, Russ. Answer my question. How do you feel about me?"

His eyes flickered uncertainly for a second, then he shrugged. "I feel good about you."

She nodded. "Good. I've heard you express more excitement about harvesting your catfish than that."

"Well, if it's excitement you want—"

"Not that kind." Carly held up her hand, despite the sudden flash of heat his suggestion stirred. "Doesn't it strike you as odd that the best description of your feelings for the woman you want to marry is good? I bet you feel good about my brothers. You feel good about your dogs. You feel good about having a beer at the end of the day."

"Carly," he began in a patient, long-suffering tone that she couldn't tolerate.

She shook her head. Quick and clean would be better. "You don't love me, do you?"

She held her breath, and a tiny, stupid part of her wished with the fervor of a toddler at Christmas.

Russ looked away, and the wish died. He didn't have to say a word.

He took her hand. "Carly, love isn't always the most important ingredient in a successful relationship. Respect, common backgrounds, common goals." He grinned. "Great sex."

She jerked away. "I'm serious, Russ. I don't think we're right for each other."

Russ narrowed his gaze, experiencing the familiar sensation of being offtrack with his plan again. He fought it. "You can trust me. I've thought this thing through. We're right for each other."

Carly shook her head sadly. "You didn't think of one thing. I need a man who loves me."

Russ saw her blinking, fighting unshed tears. He felt more helpless than a linebacker with ten bodies on top of him as he stretched to recover a fumbled ball. Hell, it was enough to make a man take up chanting.

"I need a man who's crazy about me. Crazy enough to—" She broke off, clearly searching for the right words.

"To do what?"

She raised her shoulders. "I don't know. Crazy enough to carve our initials in a tree. Crazy enough to get a tattoo of my name."

"A tattoo!" Russ snorted. "Carly, they're permanent." He tried to negotiate. "I could see initials in a tree as long as it didn't damage a good tree, but a tattoo. It's not practical."

"It's crazy," she said with a resigned I-told-you-so expression on her face.

Russ gave a heavy sigh and reached to take her in his arms, but she backed away. Her small movement of rejection pierced his thick skin, and his rumble of unease grew to something more like pain. He watched her carefully. "So what do we do now? We can't forget this weekend."

Carly crossed her arms over her chest. "No. We can't forget this"—she waved her hand—"this weekend. But we're mature adults." She began to pace, and Russ wasn't sure if she was talking to him or herself. "Even adults make mistakes. If we put it behind us—"

Her words made his blood run cold. Unable to bear the direction she was taking, he placed a hand on her shoulder to stop her. "I can't put it behind me." He turned her around and brushed a tear from her cheek. "I've felt you under me. I've touched you in ways no other man has, and I don't take it lightly."

"Oh, Russ." Carly bit her lip to hold back yet

another moan. If only he would love her. She tensed as he wrapped his arms around her.

"I've been so deep inside you I never wanted to leave."

Her heart turned inside out, and he took her mouth with the want and need of a man unwilling to be denied. It was heaven knowing how much he wanted her and hell knowing he'd never love her. Her mouth opened to his coaxing, and she instinctively responded, drawing a pleased growl from him. Her breasts strained against her bra, the tips achy from arousal, and lower, she felt a swollen emptiness where he pressed against her and rocked.

But her throat was a knot of torment at what he couldn't or wouldn't give her. Unbidden, a sob squeezed out and Russ gentled the kiss.

"I'm not ready to give you up, Carly," he muttered against her hair. "Don't close the book on us yet. We haven't given each other a fair chance." He pulled back and winced. "I don't want to make you cry, baby." The determination came back in his eyes. "Don't lock me out. Promise, Carly."

She thought she heard the faintest thread of desperation in his voice. Her mind denied it, but her heart hoped. "I can't marry you," she insisted in a not-so-steady voice.

He stopped any further protest with a firm kiss. "We'll talk about that later. Just don't shut me out."

Driving home that night, Russ assured himself that Carly would come around. She would see how right they were for each other. This was temporary, just another rut in the bumpy road to matrimony.

It came at a damned inconvenient time, however, because within a week he'd be tied up with harvesting catfish. He sensed this was a crucial time for her and thought about what he should do to ensure her commitment.

He'd like to haul her off to bed and rid her of every tiny protest in her feminine mind. But it probably wouldn't work. While men turned into mental and physical mush after sex, women tended to snap back faster with questions and emotional discussions. Russ shuddered at the thought.

He could do something romantic, he supposed, then snorted in derision. If he started acting romantic now, then Carly would expect it throughout their marriage.

He sighed as he pulled into his dirt driveway. Rationally, he was confident this quirk of Carly's would blow over.

Then he thought of her tear-filled eyes and the sob catching in her throat. "I can't marry you," she'd said. His neck felt stiff with tension. His hands tightened around the steering wheel in a death grip.

Russ cursed, pulling the truck to a stop. A tattoo of all things. All the logic in the world wasn't going to get rid of the uneasy dread that sat in his stomach. He looked at his house, dark and empty. It needed Carly's laughter to make it a home. He wondered for an agonizing moment if all his planning and wanting had turned into something bigger and more frightening. Something emotional, God help him.

"The roses were beautiful, Russ," Carly said in a quiet voice, when he appeared in the doorway below deck.

Walking forward, Russ heard the warmth in her voice and felt his pulse skip a beat. "Glad you liked them," he said gruffly, then took her hand and brushed a kiss over it. She blushed, and he was infinitely glad he'd sent those roses.

In concession to the heat, she wore a lavender tank top and white shorts that showed the length of her tanned shapely legs. Her hair was tousled and her face smudged, and Russ could only think of how much fun it would be to join her in a shower and clean every inch of her.

A cough broke the moment, and Russ noticed Troy behind Carly.

"Hi, Russ," Troy said in a singsong voice. Then he fluttered his hands as if plucking imaginary harp strings.

Russ nodded stiffly. "Troy. What are you doing here?"

"Jarod and Garth skipped off to the beach, so I'm helping out my baby sister with *our* riverboat." He gave Russ a broad wink.

Russ stifled the urge to roll his eyes. "You can go do something you want to do, now. I'll help her." He looked around, noticing life vests thrown all over the place. "What happened?"

"Coast guard inspection," Carly said as she picked up one and put it away. "These guys get their grins by pulling everything out and leaving it as messy as possible. I've got a special group coming for lunch tomorrow, so I need to get it all put away."

"Are they paying?" Troy asked.

Carly paused, then continued. "No, it's a charity."

"Carly, you gotta cut that out. You'll never make any money if you keep giving these free cruises. Who is it this time? The Ladies Auxiliary?"

"It's not the Ladies Auxiliary," she assured him patiently. But Russ heard the tension in her tone. Rolling up his sleeves, he studied her.

"Then who is it?" Troy asked impertinently.

She didn't answer for a full moment, putting away another life vest. "It's a support group for children who have lost a parent."

The simple statement rendered the two men silent. Troy stared at Carly with his mouth open, and Russ watched the calm expression on her face. Underneath the calm, he sensed turmoil. He frowned.

Recovering his voice, Troy cleared his throat and shrugged. "Well, I, uh, guess that's okay. After all, it's only one time." He looked at Russ. "If you're gonna help Carly, I think I'll head on back to the farm. See you later." He awkwardly planted a kiss on Carly's cheek and left.

Carly just looked after him and sighed.

"You heard from the bank yet?"

She nodded. "They won't give me the money."

When he saw the disappointment on her face, he felt guilty over his extreme relief. "Well, if you can't buy out your brothers, have you thought about finding a silent partner?"

She looked confused. "But who? I'd need someone with enough money who'd let me handle things without interference."

Russ wanted to shout, *Me!* Instead, he kept his voice lowered. "There must be someone in town who you can trust. He would have to have a business of his own, so he wouldn't be tempted to meddle in yours. He would have to be confident in your business abilities. It probably wouldn't hurt if you'd known him a long time, so neither of you would be surprised." Russ felt sure he was drawing an accurate picture of himself.

"Hmmm," she said cocking her head to one side. "I can't really think of—" Her face cleared. "Wait a minute. What about the director from National Electronics? I haven't known him very long, but he'd be perfect. He's got money and he's focused on his own business, and he seems to like me."

Russ gazed at the ceiling, silently begging for mercy.

"Russ," Carly said as she hugged him, "that's a great idea."

Caught between the pleasure of feeling her pressed against him and the frustration of being waylaid again, Russ groaned. "I wouldn't rush into anything. After all, you don't really know this guy. He could end up being worse than your brothers."

"I'll think it over first," she assured him. "But it's a great idea. Thanks."

Then she kissed him. She'd probably intended it as a light gesture of appreciation, but Russ's arms instinctively tightened around her. He nudged her lips open with his until he could taste her, and her sweetness and warmth sent a surge of heat throughout his blood. She squeezed his shoulders, and he explored her silky mouth with his tongue. By the time he pulled away, he felt as though he were missing one lung and his jeans didn't fit right.

Carly looked a little shell-shocked herself. Russ took a deep breath and grinned slowly. "You're welcome."

As the hot afternoon gave way to a warm, humid evening, Carly felt increasingly distracted. Part of her wanted to throw Russ overboard and scream, "I love you and you don't love me. Leave me alone!" Another part of her liked having him around. He was attentive and watchful in a way that made her heart swell.

He'd taken off his white shirt hours earlier. Every movement accentuated the strength of his muscled chest, ribs, and flat belly. She was reminded of the time she'd spent exploring his body. She remembered the way his stomach quivered when she'd run her fingers across it. She'd pressed her mouth against his navel, intending to taste him, but he'd pulled her up and busied her mouth with his.

"Carly, where are you?" Russ asked, leaning over her.

She blinked and shook off the images, shifting on the wooden bench. Pure craziness! She'd decided to take a short break and ended up thinking about Russ. "Right here," she said, offering him a can of soda. "It was nice of you to help today. You really didn't have to."

"Yes I did." He straddled the bench and took a long drink.

Carly watched his throat work while he swallowed the cool liquid, and felt her own mouth go dry. This wasn't right, she thought. She was supposed to be backing away from Russ, not fixating on his body. She moved to stand, but he pulled her back down.

"Tell me about this group that's coming tomorrow. How'd you find them?"

"They found me." She felt him lift his hand to her hair and sift his fingers through it. The motion was simple, yet mesmerizing. She sighed. "They're associated with Central Tennessee's Women and Children's Center, and they sent out a letter asking for volunteers to head up their different support groups."

"So, are you gonna volunteer?"

His low, soothing voice overrode her usual discomfort in discussing this particular subject. She shook her head. "I don't think I could. I'd probably only make matters worse if I told them my story."

His hands moved to her shoulders. "I thought you handled it real well. You didn't cry very much."

"Only at night," she murmured. An evening breeze brushed over her, and with the heat of Russ's warm, solid chest at her back, she felt safe. "At first, Daniel would come and try to comfort me, but Eunice made him stop. She said it would spoil me. I'm not sure Daddy ever heard me."

His hands paused for a second, then he gently brushed his fingers around her neck and under her jaw. "Eunice was a tough woman."

Carly closed her eyes and nodded. "I tried to get her to like me, but there was no pleasing her. It was hard for her to look at me. Hard for Daddy too," she admitted. "You know, Eunice was in a rough situation with eight kids to manage. And Dad never got over my mother. Eunice knew that. I think it made her bitter. And looking at a miniature of the woman who held my father's heart must have been torture. But . . ." She paused, remembering her confusion, the sting of rejection.

"But?" he prompted gently.

"But I was just a little girl and I didn't understand what was going on until I was sixteen or seventeen. I was sure there was something wrong with me."

"Don't think that. It wasn't you."

His voice was reassuring, but the memories bubbled inside her like a witch's cauldron. It was unfinished business that could never be resolved. She fought against the unsatisfied need inside her.

She turned to face Russ. "She just couldn't love me. That's why we can't—"

Shaking his head, he covered her mouth with his hand. "Eunice was bitter. It's not the same thing at all, Carly."

She grabbed his shoulders. "But it feels the same." She thought of his divorce but couldn't bring herself to say it.

"It's not. You're gonna have to trust me on this." Then he caught her jaw and lifted it, and stared into her eyes as if he were making a commitment.

His callused thumbs moved gently over her cheeks and eyelids, caressing her, speaking without words. In a slow, careful motion, he lowered his head and cherished her lips with his mouth and tongue. She'd exposed her secrets, and his tender touches weakened and nurtured her. There was a sweetness about him that moved her until it hurt.

When his hands skirted down her neck to her breasts and he changed the angle of his kiss, she tried to pull away. "This is wrong. We need to stop," she said, breathlessly, and turned her head from him. She stiffened her resolve.

"Let me do this. I, I need to."

The hesitation in his voice vanquished her resistance. She wished he'd used any word but need because the idea of Russ needing her made her head swim. Need was deeper than want, closer to love.

"I need to do this for you, Carly. Now." He brushed his lips against her hair. "Tonight."

If he'd ordered or demanded, she could have found the strength to walk away, but there was something rich and unselfish in his manner that asked, yet didn't insist. She was helpless against it. "Oh, Russ," she murmured.

Beneath her palms, his chest expanded in a deep breath. "Let me take care of you."

And because Carly had always been recklessly hopeful, she pretended that Russ loved her. It was easy in the dark, with his warm hands and mouth caressing her. The secret fantasy made her weightless. She felt the slide of his fingers on the inside of her tank straps against her skin, edging slowly closer to her breasts, and she shivered.

"Cold?" he murmured, dropping light teasing kisses behind her ear, as his fingers fell just short of her turgid nipples.

Carly shook her head and arched against him. Her breasts were already heavy. When he finally touched her, she sighed in relief. He rolled the peaks between his thumb and forefinger, praising her response. A restlessness deep inside her grew, and she wanted to be close to him.

She pressed an openmouthed kiss against the throat that had captivated her earlier. She touched it with her tongue and earned a shudder of male approval. Russ pulled her onto his lap, pushed up her tank top, and rested his cheek against her heart.

Her breath caught. The gesture was so artless and intimate. Then he skimmed his mouth across her breast to her nipple and suckled. Carly could have wept.

Her vision blurred as he moved his mouth from one breast to the other, gently nipping and flicking his tongue over her. One of his hands cupped her hips, rubbing her against his hard denim-covered arousal, back and forth until she was liquid heat between her thighs, ready and wanting.

She trailed her hands down his chest, past his rib cage, past his abdomen, to his belt buckle.

He shook his head. "Just this once, trust me." Then he captured her hands and turned her around so that her rear end was wedged against his thighs. She squirmed in protest and he groaned. "Give me a break, lady."

"But, what—"

"Shh." He nuzzled her neck and lazily skimmed his fingers up one of her thighs, underneath her roomy shorts. He lifted the elastic barrier of her panties and found where she was achingly, embarrassingly moist for him. She turned her head into his shoulder. Her skin was so hot, she felt like a branding iron.

"You're sweet," he muttered as he palmed her, "and warm. I want to do so many things to you, I don't know where to start."

Carly tried to say something, but her mind went blank when he gently slipped his finger inside her. A moan escaped her lips as he probed and explored her. With masculine fascination, he stretched and coddled her, praising her femininity until she bit her lip against the tension. Each thrust took her closer and closer to release until she was twisting her head from side to side.

"What is it?" he asked in a low voice.

"I need," she gasped as he pressed another finger inside her. "I need to do something. I need to kiss you, to touch you."

He nudged her head around and she found his mouth, kissing him and tasting him. He moved his thumb against her swollen bud, and she jerked as the ripples began. They consumed her like a roaring fire in a tunnel. She bucked, whimpering into his mouth, feeling the uneven spasms go on and on until at last the surge passed and she was left with warmth and weak relief.

It took a couple of moments and several shakily drawn breaths before Carly realized that although Russ's hands were now soothing, he was still hard with arousal. She turned in his arms and looked into his unreadable eyes. Confused and unsure of what to do, she slid her hands down to his belly and worried the edge of his jeans with her fingers. When he stilled her hands, she was overcome with bewilderment.

"Don't you want to, I mean, you're still . . ." She sighed in frustration. "We're not finished, are we?"

He brought her hands to his mouth and kissed them. "Yeah, I want to," he reassured her. "Yeah, I'm still hard. But we're finished for tonight." He put her hands on his cheeks and closed his eyes, savoring her touch. He tried to sort it out, but it was too profound having Carly in his arms tonight. It was scary. "I don't know how to explain it, but I needed to give you this tonight. It wasn't sex. It was something else." He opened his eyes. "Are you okay?"

Carly had never felt more vulnerable. "I'm okay, just a little embarrassed."

He shook his head. "No embarrassment allowed. You were beautiful. You are beautiful." He leaned forward and kissed her forehead.

And to Carly, it was *almost* as if he loved her.

Nine

"People say it all the time and it doesn't mean a thing." Russ jerked his car to a stop. He didn't understand it, wouldn't attempt to articulate it, but after being with Carly, he felt as though he were walking around stark naked. Sharing her vulnerability left him feeling defenseless, and the unfamiliar sensation confused and agitated him. How the hell had they gotten on this subject on the short drive from the riverboat? He couldn't blame Carly. She looked a little off kilter herself.

"Some people mean it," Carly insisted.

Disgusted, he shook his head. "This is crazy."

"Then, maybe I'm crazy." She met his gaze with turbulent violet eyes. "Maybe that means I'm not the right woman for you. Maybe you need someone who doesn't care whether you love her or not."

Fury raced through him. He clenched his jaw. "I know my own mind. I know who the right woman is."

She set her chin. "Well I'm not sure." Then she got out of the car and slammed the door behind her.

Russ swore in exasperation, going after her. "Carly, wait up. For Pete's sake, what happened? One minute you're coming apart in my arms—"

"Don't remind me," she muttered, stomping up the stairs.

"Remind you!" Why didn't she just stab him? Russ swore again and rushed ahead, beating her to her door. "Something happened between us tonight. Something special. And you want to forget it?"

Carly crossed her arms over her chest. "It was special," she admitted, "but there needs to be more."

He took a deep breath. They needed to slow down. He'd lost control. That's why they were in this mess. He needed to think logically. There was a practical solution to this, and he'd find it. "What are you talking about?"

"I'm talking about feelings. Not just mine. Yours. I sat there and spilled my guts tonight, and you did something beautiful afterward. But do you realize I can count on one finger the number of times you've ever discussed something that was emotionally important to you?"

Russ felt an immediate ripple of discomfort. He rubbed the back of his neck with his hand. The idea of discussing his emotions made him itchy. He'd rather clean a truckload of fish. He looked at her face, full of vulnerability and determination. She wasn't going to budge on this. Maybe it wouldn't be so bad, he told himself. Either way, he had no choice.

"Okay," he conceded finally. "What do you want to know?"

She licked her lips and appeared to muster her courage. "I want to know how you feel about your first marriage."

Russ's wall of protection immediately rose higher than Jacob's ladder. "That was over years ago. It's a closed book."

A long silence followed, and Russ realized he'd made a mistake. She wanted him to bare his soul, but God help him he just couldn't. To discuss the biggest failure of his life with the woman he wanted to marry was untenable. He searched her eyes for compassion. He prayed for understanding. But she looked away.

"Thanks for helping with *Matilda's Dream*, Russ." She collected the keys from her purse.

He was being dismissed, he realized with a twisting ache in his gut. "Carly, we can talk later. I'll be harvesting for the next few days, but after that . . ."

She gave a noncommittal shrug, and when he sensed her disappointment, he was stricken with regret. She looked disillusioned, and he felt guilty, helpless, and angry all at once.

"Good night, Russ."

He watched her turn her back and walk into her apartment, resisting the urge to reach for her. What could he say or do that would help? "Good night, Carly," he murmured to her closed door.

Carly stared at her bedroom ceiling. She closed her eyes and waited for her body to get smart and go to sleep. She concentrated very hard for two minutes. When her thoughts turned to Russ, her eyes flew open again.

She had to do something soon. They couldn't continue this way. It was wrong for Russ to expect her to brush aside her concerns about love just as it was wrong for her to expect him to change. She ran her hand across her forehead and squelched the futile wish that things could be different.

The telephone rang, breaking the silence. Her heart raced and she looked at the clock. After midnight. No good calls ever came after midnight.

Stumbling over the bedcovers, she jerked up the phone. "Hello."

"It's Russ. There was a fire in Daniel's barn. He's gonna be okay, but we're at the emergency room. He burned his hands."

Carly's thoughts tripped over one another. "How bad are his hands? Are you sure he's okay? What about the animals?"

"The barn burned to the ground, and I had to put down one of the horses."

"Oh, no."

"Daniel's got first-degree burns." His voice was gruff. "He'll be wearing bandages for a while."

Carly went numb at the thought of Daniel's injuries. She'd lost too much at an early age to take an accident of this magnitude in stride. "I'll be there as soon as I can," she said, groping for a pair of jeans.

"Carly, we don't need any more accidents tonight. You sound kinda shaky. Do you want me to come and get you?"

"No." Her nerveless fingers fumbled with the zipper. "I need to get there. You're sure he's okay?"

"He's okay. I swear." Russ paused. "Be careful."

"I will." She hung up the phone, jerked off her nightgown, and pulled on a T-shirt. She grabbed a pair of shoes and her keys and ran to the car.

Within minutes, she arrived at the small local hospital. She looked for Russ and instead found

Troy. Troy was shaken and covered in soot, but otherwise unhurt. "You're a mess," he said.

"You smell horrible," she said, tears of relief filling her eyes. "Where's Daniel?"

"This way. They gave him something for the pain, so he's out like a light." He led her down the hall to where Daniel lay sleeping.

Carly felt for his heartbeat. It was ridiculous, but necessary to her. She touched his forehead and gently kissed him on the cheek. Then she backed away and willed herself to calm down. "Do you know how it happened?"

Troy shook his head. "Russ was pulling Daniel out when I got there. The horses were going crazy. Sal was screaming. She was in such pain, Russ had to shoot her. After that, Russ started yelling at Daniel and me to get back and let the fire department handle it."

Carly's stomach felt like lead. "Where is Russ?"

"As soon as he called you, he was out of here like a shot. He went back to take the horses over to his place. He barely let them bandage his arm."

"He's hurt? He didn't tell me that on the phone."

Troy snorted. "He was probably too busy giving orders. He told me if I didn't stay here with Daniel tonight, he'd sic the Ladies Auxiliary on me."

"A fate worse than death?" Carly took his arm and coaxed him out of the room. She knew Troy hated hospitals. His contrariness hid a tender, caring heart. When they were little, he'd always been the one to sneak an extra scoop of ice cream or piece of candy for Carly. "Why don't you go to my apartment and take a shower and get some sleep? You look like you need it more than I do."

"Is that an insult?"

"No," she said, wrapping her arms around her most obstinate brother. "It's my way of saying I love you."

He let out a deep breath and squeezed her. "Same here. I'll, uh, I'll take you up on your offer. You sure you don't mind?"

"I'm sure," Carly said, but at the same time she wondered about Russ.

"Garth and Jarod picked a hell of a time for a beach trip," Troy said, shaking his head.

"Yeah. At least they'll be back on Sunday."

"I guess Russ and I can pick up the slack till then." Troy bussed her on the cheek. "See you tomorrow."

She noticed the way he relied on Russ without question. Returning to Daniel's room, Carly remembered Russ's harvest plans. She spent the better part of the night recalling how they'd last parted and wondering if it burdened Russ as much as it did her.

The next morning, Carly drove Daniel home and settled him in bed with a big glass of ginger ale and a straw. While he slept, she made a quick trip over to Russ's and found him and his crew stretching a hydraulic seine across one of his ponds.

Russ nodded at her when she waved, but kept on working. "How's Daniel?"

"Tired and crabby." Even at this early hour, the sun beat down without an ounce of pity. He'd tied a white handkerchief around his head to keep the sweat from his eyes. She wished she'd brought him something to drink. She noted the stark contrast between his white bandage and tanned arm. "You didn't tell me you got hurt."

He shrugged. "Didn't seem important at the time."

Her heart twisted. How could he think it wouldn't be important? Then she remembered that she hadn't asked him anything about himself during their brief phone call the night before. "When did you get to bed?"

"No time," he said, then called out an order to one of his crew.

"Well, don't worry about coming over to Daniel's tonight. You've got enough on your plate, and if you're harvesting tomorrow, you'll need your rest."

"I can handle it."

Exasperation spun inside her. "You don't have to. We'll find someone else. I know you had to shoot Sal last night, and you probably need—"

"Save it, Carly," Russ cut in and looked at her for the first time. "I don't need the mothering routine from you. I'm fine."

It took a full minute for her to catch her breath. God, it hurt to have him shut her out. Instinct had pride, then anger covering her like a shield. She pressed her lips together in a bitter smile. "Excuse me. I made a mistake and forgot you're not human." Then she turned and left, barely noticing the string of curses Russ let out before she closed her car door.

It required all of Carly's persuasive abilities, but by noon, Sara was serving Daniel his lunch and Carly was helping serve the children-who-have-lost-a-parent group their lunch. She shoved Russ and his cool attitude firmly from her mind. Every time she thought about his closed expression and his flat tone of voice, she felt as though a lash were cutting across her heart. It hurt to smile, but she managed.

Augusta Winfree, the leader of the group, was a

pretty blond woman in her thirties with an easy smile, generous laughter, and compassionate hazel eyes. She was one of the most feminine women Carly had ever seen, yet the children called her Gus. "I think they're having a good time," she said to Carly as they watched the waitstaff lead the children in the hokeypokey.

"Good. You'll have to come back." The close-knit group made her curious. "They seem so well adjusted. Do you meet every week?"

Augusta nodded. "And everybody has two buddies they can call if things start getting rough."

Carly was amazed. "This is wonderful. I wish they'd had something like this when I was a child."

"You lost a parent when you were little?"

"Both," Carly said simply. Her losses were a sore spot that had never completely healed. She tended to handle the subject gingerly to avoid extra pain. Carly shook off a quick stab, and gently smiled at the solemn, dark-haired little girl who approached Augusta. Carly felt a rush of déjà vu. That little girl could have been her fifteen years ago.

"Need a hug?" Augusta asked. Not waiting for an answer, she pulled the little girl onto her lap and squeezed her. Augusta cuddled her for a few minutes, then the little girl returned to the group. "That was Jacey. Her mother died three months ago. She doesn't want to talk much yet. She just wants the hugs."

Carly marveled at what a special service the group provided. "What do you do at the meetings?"

"We always have cookies or ice cream," Augusta said in a mock serious tone. "I insist on it. Sometimes we have social outings, like pizza parties, or swimming. Other nights when I have enough volunteers, we break into groups and deal with feelings. We draw faces, write stories. The stories tend to be autobiographical. We work very hard to teach the children not to blame themselves. There's so much guilt."

Carly nodded, remembering. "You're right about that."

"We always need more volunteers."

Carly shook her head. "Not yet. I've got some other things to settle first." She hesitated, thinking of Russ. "Maybe after that."

"Sounds like you're wishing something in your life were different."

Surprised, Carly raised her eyebrows. "You're very perceptive."

Augusta gave a wry smile. "It's a gift. Anyway, that's one of the other things we do. We talk about wishes for what might have been. Sometimes people get stuck on that instead of going forward and trying to make their wishes come true." She shrugged. "It's not just children who've lost a parent. It can be someone who's become disappointed or disillusioned by any number of things, like job loss, divorce."

Augusta sounded as though she'd had personal experience with grief. Carly wondered about the source of it, but didn't ask, sensing Augusta's need for privacy.

"When people are hurt, they get scared and sometimes they're so busy protecting themselves, they forget how to open up."

Her observation brought a spasm of pain. Augusta was talking about Russ. He'd been hurt and now he was protecting himself. What would it take for him to open up again? Was it even possible? she wondered with a despair so strong, her chest hurt. "How do you help someone like that?" she murmured.

Augusta gestured toward the group of children. Her expression softened. "You have to be patient," she said. "And *very* stubborn."

Carly stared at Augusta, seeing hope and determination. Maybe that's what it would take for Russ to open up. Augusta's words took root within her. The seed was planted. Well, at least half a seed. Patience had never been Carly's long suit, but she could do stubborn like nobody's business.

Thursday night, Russ dragged himself up the wooden steps to his front door and simply leaned against it for a moment. Lord, he was tired. He wondered what little surprise would be sitting on his kitchen table tonight. It had been a homemade loaf of bread the first night, strawberry preserves the next, and last night there'd been a squat glass of his favorite whiskey.

He had strong suspicions about who was leaving him the gifts and it wasn't the Ladies Auxiliary. He'd called her a few times and left messages on her answering machine, but between the harvest and Daniel's accident he'd had no time to seek her out.

He wished they didn't have this misunderstanding between them. After sharing so much with her, then leaving her, he'd been carrying two unbearable aches, one behind his breastbone, the other in his pants. Both were persistent, and Russ was convinced that Carly was the best person to take care of all his aches. He wished she were in there, waiting for him, ready for him. Russ gave a dry chuckle. Hell, he was so tired, he wouldn't be able to do anything if she were there.

He shook his head and shoved open the door. When he reached the kitchen, he stopped and stared at the table. *Meet me at the swimming pond,* a note written in feminine script said. *And bring the apples.*

Russ raised an eyebrow skeptically. He put his hands in his pocket and looked at the red apples beside the note. He couldn't stop the bubble of laughter building in his chest. But he strangled on his sense of humor, coughing violently, when he saw what was behind those red apples. Three plastic packets of prophylactics.

"She's lost it," Russ muttered. She could drown in that pond at night. How long had she been waiting? he wondered. He crammed the rubbers in his pocket and stalked out the door. He grabbed a flashlight from his truck and took off through the woods.

"Carly," he yelled as he got closer to the swimming pond. "I'm gonna kill—" He walked straight into a skirt hanging from a tree. His blood pressure rose fifty points. Another few steps and he found a tank top. His gaze landed on the bra clinging decoratively to a tree limb, and he started to sweat.

He struggled for oxygen, inhaling her sultry scent as he clutched her clothes in his hands. Two more steps and his flashlight found the shiny, slippery-looking triangle of her panties. He thought about leaving them there on that bush, but he couldn't resist rubbing the silky material between his fingers. It reminded him of the last time he'd held and touched her, how soft and moist she'd been. He couldn't hold back a moan.

"Carly!" he yelled, stumbling the last few feet to the pond. "Have you lost your mind?" He heard a splashing noise and turned his head, finding her. She was a water nymph with black hair and glowing skin. Moonlight shone on her face and pale shoulders.

"Come on in," she called, smiling. "The water's fine."

"What's gotten into you? It's almost eleven o'clock."

"I know. If you'd taken much longer, my skin would have started to prune." She bobbed underneath the surface and rose again, shaking her head. "I'm just inviting you for a friendly swim. Come on."

Frustration and good sense warred inside him. "I've got too much work to be out here fooling around."

"You've been working too hard. You need to take a break. I'm following your example. That's what friends are for. Isn't that what you said when you kidnapped me?"

Russ shifted his feet and exhaled heavily. "That was different."

"How?" Carly lazily slid onto her back and floated. While her feet sank beneath the surface, the water flirted with her torso. Her firm breasts were revealed, the tips like small raspberries on cream.

His jeans nearly split in two. Russ licked his lips, feeling his resolve wane. "Get out," he said before he gave in.

She giggled, then rolled over and he caught sight of her gorgeous derriere. "Oh Lord," he murmured weakly. He closed his eyes. "Get out," he called in his most intimidating voice. Then he glared at her.

Carly just threw him a siren's smile. *"Come and get me."*

That tore it. Russ mentally waved the white flag of surrender. How much could a man endure? He figured he'd already broken the record for most persistent arousal. Heedless of buttons flying into the grass, he ripped off his shirt, unfastened his jeans and eased them over his distended manhood. He kicked off his shoes, socks, and jeans.

Carly wolf-whistled. "Don't forget the apple!"

She was a wicked witch, he thought. And she was going to be his wife if he had to lock her in his house for the next fifty years. Russ finally cracked a smile. He shook his head and started walking. "It's not easy getting those on in the water, Carly."

"You're a talented man."

"It can be tricky." He splashed into the pond until his knees and waist were covered by the cool water.

She flutter-kicked closer to him. "I'll help," she offered. His breath caught when she touched his jaw and looked at him with concern etched across her delicate features. "How are you?"

His insides went gushy, but his body stayed hard. Though his need was fierce, her tenderness chipped away at his irritation. He pulled her into his arms and pressed her cool breasts to his heated chest. "Okay."

"I've missed you," Carly murmured. She kissed his neck and suckled on his earlobe.

Russ nudged her head back and took her sweet mouth, sipping from it like a starving man. He was so hungry for her, his body shook. He rubbed her shoulder and felt goose bumps on her skin. "You're freezing. Let's get out of here."

"Not yet." Carly fluttered her hands over his shoulders. She averted her head. The vixen had turned shy, he thought. He'd trade an entire harvest for what was inside her mind at this minute. He watched her take a deep breath. "There's something I've never done, and I was kinda hoping you'd . . ."

Curious, Russ cupped her chin and raised it so he could see her. "What?"

"Well, I want to"—she lowered her voice to a whisper—"do it in the water."

His insides twisted. "Honey, I wish we could, but I left the protection in my pocket."

She bit her lip. "Well, could we do it for just a minute?"

Russ groaned. She didn't know what she was asking. A minute was all it would take for him right now. But he couldn't find the wherewithal to resist her. "You're gonna kill me," he muttered before he kissed her hotly, savagely. It required every ounce of his self-discipline, but he skimmed his hands over her, reacquainting himself with her curves, arousing her. He played with her until they were both so hot, he expected steam to rise from their skin.

Then he lifted her, and she wrapped her legs around his waist. The water lapped around them, cushioning their movements. He slowly penetrated her until she gloved him. The connection drew a soft moan from her lips, and her face glowed with his possession of her.

He closed his eyes and shuddered. Sixty seconds, he told himself. *I can do this for sixty seconds.* But then she moved. "Stop," he said tightly. "Don't move." In spite of the cool water, he felt sweat bead on his forehead.

She curled herself around him and made love to his mouth, nipping and sucking on his lips. Her beaded nipples teased his chest, while her belly rubbed against his. Her thighs were a silken pleasure, putting him somewhere between heaven and hell. He resisted his need to caress her, knowing if he did, everything would be over in less than a minute.

"That's it," he said, gritting his teeth. He drew away, feeling his body scream in frustration, then carried her from the pond to his discarded clothes.

His hands were immediately all over her with his mouth following suit. He remembered the sensitive spot behind her ear. He remembered how she loved the rasp of his cheek against her shoulder. He remembered that her skin rippled when he skimmed his fingers low over her abdomen. He generously exploited her senses, and challenged her sanity.

Carly gasped when he gently parted her legs with one of his knees. "Russ," she whispered. His heat took the chill from her skin. The sky was a spinning kaleidoscope of a bright, full moon and sparkling stars.

"I've wanted you every night since that weekend we spent together," he muttered against her neck, visibly trying to slow down.

He nuzzled his way down her chest until his hot mouth found a nipple. He tugged and she felt it everywhere, from her head that seemed as light as air, to her mouth that suddenly went dry when his questing fingers found her aching femininity, to her toes that curled in pure pleasure.

"Russ," she managed to say in an unsteady voice, "you're making my head spin."

He switched breasts and chuckled. The vibration of his mouth jolted her like a bare live wire. "Go ahead and spin."

She fought against his madness. "No. There's one more thing—" She broke off when he pressed that talented mouth to her belly button. Then she shook her head and grabbed his hair. "I mean it, Russ," she pleaded.

He stopped and raised his head close to hers. His bottomless brown eyes were full of passion. "What is it?"

"There's one more thing I want to do tonight that I've never done before." She gave a gentle push, the gesture asking him to give her free rein.

He turned and caught her face between his hands. "You know you belong to me."

Carly swallowed hard. "It's time you learned you belong to me." She shook free of his hands and pressed openmouthed kisses down his chest until she was the one flicking her tongue over his belly button. He jerked, but she continued. She allowed only a second of uncertainty.

Then she kissed him intimately.

"Oh, my God," he said in a rough voice.

She tasted him with her tongue and learned his male texture, satin wrapped around steel. He was shaking. His abandoned response made her feel deliciously sexy. She liked the feeling so much, she got more daring. She opened her mouth, enclosing him, taking him in a rhythmic movement until he swore and pulled her away.

He breathed harshly, and his eyes were wild. "I can't take any more. I need you."

Her spirit soared at his obvious, overwhelming need for her. She knew it was only for her.

In seconds he protected her, and turned her over. Carly didn't know who was more relieved when he sheathed himself inside her. They both moaned.

It wasn't long before she felt the beginning shudders while she watched his eyes. They glowed like fire, and his face was taut with arousal. He thrust and she arched. Then, fast and furious, the peak came, sweeping both of them into its cyclone strength. Afterward, she was so overcome, she wept while he trembled.

Ten

The next morning all the prophylactics were gone.

Carly untangled herself from Russ's arms and kissed him good-bye with a promise to meet him at his house for an early dinner before the evening cruise.

She hummed her way through the day, thinking things felt differently to her. She was hopeful, truly hopeful.

That afternoon they enjoyed cold sandwiches and conversation until Russ's phone rang. Propping his feet on a kitchen chair, he talked to a distributor and rolled an apple across the table to Carly.

Carly caught it and smiled. She watched the crinkles around his eyes as he grinned in return. Her heart tripped. Could she possibly be happier than she was at this very minute? Carly rolled the apple back.

"Yeah, that's right, David," Russ said as he began tossing it into the air and catching it. He pointed meaningfully to his lap, obviously wanting her to join him.

She slowly shook her head.

She saw his eyes darken with retaliatory promise. He tossed the apple again. "Uh-huh, thanks for checking."

Before he could react, Carly snitched the apple midair and took a bite.

"Anytime, bye now." Russ hung up the phone. "Are you *teasing* me?"

Carly batted her eyes in innocence. "Who me? Tease the catfish king?"

He rose and stalked her around the table. "You're playing a dangerous game."

Carly scooted around a chair. "I'll take my chances." Then she stopped short, because she suddenly realized she wasn't kidding. She'd be willing to take her chances with Russ. Forever kind of chances. It was an awakening that somehow managed to imbed her feelings about Russ more deeply at the same time that it shook her foundation.

"Gotcha!" He wrapped his arms around her.

Carly stared blankly at Russ, pulling back. She could have used a moment alone to come to grips with this, she thought. "Here," she said and put the apple to his mouth so he could take a bite. "You can have it."

Russ refused the bite but took the apple and looked at her in bewilderment. "If I could spend five minutes in your head . . ."

"You'd get lost. Remember? I don't do straight-line thinking."

Russ chuckled and slung his arm around her shoulder. "Let's go out on the porch." He stopped.

"But first, I want you to look at the kitchen and your shirt."

Carly slit her eyes at him. And he thought *her* train of thought was convoluted.

"You match." He pointed to the yellow stripe in her shirt. "Yellow on your shirt and in my kitchen."

She nodded, but didn't have a clue what he was discussing. "Uh-huh."

"And the green stripe goes with my den."

Carly waited silently. She'd check his forehead for fever in a minute.

"And we already know you go perfectly in my bedroom," he said as he ushered her to the porch.

"I'm not wearing aqua," she felt compelled to point out.

He pulled her down beside him on the sliding porch swing. "You go perfectly when you wear nothing. Your shoes look great on my bedroom carpet. You match this house and me so well, you should stay here permanently."

His point finally dawned. "Think so, huh?"

His grin fell, dispelling the light mood. His eyes were serious, so filled with somber commitment that her chest felt crowded and achy. He took her hand and looked at it. She couldn't help but tremble.

"Gwen," he began, and Carly felt her stomach take a dive. Gwen was his first wife.

"She was a homecoming queen, and she chased me up and down campus." He shrugged. "She was just a freshman and I was a senior when we met."

Carly held her breath then slowly released it. *Close your mouth, you ninny. This is what you've been asking for.*

"Gwen used to say that being with me was the most important thing in her life. Marrying me would be a dream come true. I probably should have known better, but Dad had just died and Mom was making plans to move to Florida."

He squeezed her fingers, frowning. "It's easy to fall for a beautiful woman who says all the right things."

His disappointment was etched in his face and written in his tone. A flare of futile jealousy burned within her.

"Pretty soon, the tide turned, and I was chasing her, begging her to quit college at the end of the year to marry me. We married in June. She hated living on a farm. She missed the frat parties and the football games. I didn't want to face the fact that it wasn't working out. She left on Christmas Eve." His bitter laugh was rusty. "I must've stayed drunk for a solid week."

Carly swallowed. "Did you ever try to get her back?"

Russ met her gaze. "Just once, but she'd already seen a lawyer. She wanted a divorce."

"Must have hurt."

Russ nodded. "Like hell." He turned his head thoughtfully to one side. "I thought I'd never get married again till you. I wanted nothing to do with it."

"I'm young," Carly pointed out quietly.

He cupped her chin. "You've had your share of losses. It's made you strong. You're the most loving woman I've ever met." He took a deep breath. "What I"—he hesitated—"feel for you is deeper than anything I've felt for any other woman."

Tears backed up in Carly's eyes. It wasn't *I love you*, but it was darned close. "Oh, Russ."

"I want to spend the rest of my life trying to figure out the way you think. I want to be with you when you make a huge success of that riverboat." He stroked her cheek and painted a picture for her. "I want us to trade secrets and make babies together. I want to fight and make up, but only with you." He lowered his voice to a deep, low rumble that seemed to come from his very heart. "I joke about it, but, Carly, I want you with me forever."

She looked into his clear brown eyes and saw only honesty. Her resistance crumbled. She loved him more than she'd dreamed possible. Carly threw her arms around his neck and hugged him tight, feeling both his strength and exhale of surprise.

He ruffled the hair at her nape with one hand and wrapped his other hand around her waist. "How long are you gonna make me wait, lady?"

Her heart seemed to burst. "Not anymore, Russ," she whispered. "No more waiting."

He stiffened and put a little space between them. He stared into her eyes. He must have been looking for a sign and found it. His hands were bands of steel encircling her arms. "You're sure? Did I hear you right?"

Carly nodded. "I'm sure."

In one exuberant movement, Russ stood and pulled Carly with him. He let out a rebel yell, and the dogs started barking. The porch and trees blurred together as he spun her around and around.

Finally, he stopped and just stared at her. His smile could have lit up the whole state of Tennessee. He kissed her and allowed her to slide down the length of his body. By the time he broke the kiss, Carly was dizzy with happiness. She barely comprehended what he was saying.

"We'll have the ceremony next week," he announced. "To hell with waiting till September."

Carly nodded weakly, struggling for her equilibrium.

"And we'll get your ring now. The jeweler's still open, and I want you to help pick it out. Then we'll tell your brothers."

Carly nodded again, then remembered her cruise and shook her head.

Russ paused, studying her. "No?"

"I've got a cruise tonight. It starts in—" She checked her watch and made a face. "I should probably leave now."

"I forgot," Russ said.

Carly laughed. "So did I."

Consternation crossed his face. "It's a hell of a time to watch you ride off into the sunset. I'll drive you. We can talk on the way." He dug car keys out of his pocket and guided her toward his truck. "I'll pick you up after the cruise and bring you back here."

"You don't have to," Carly said when he opened the door for her.

"Yes I do. Your car will be here." He shortened the distance between their faces. "Besides, we've got something to celebrate tonight and I won't have a minute alone with you once we tell your brothers."

Carly's heart turned a little flip. He brushed his mouth against hers in a firm, possessive kiss that hinted more would come later. She managed to get in the truck and sit down.

"You'll need to give notice for your apartment lease," Russ pointed out as he drove toward town. "Do you have any idea who you'll want to give you away at the wedding?"

Carly thought of her seven brothers and how special each of them was to her. She shook her head.

"I don't know. I wouldn't want any of them to feel left out."

Russ chuckled. "You could always ask all of them. By the way, is tonight's cruise for anyone special?"

"National Electronics. They'll be booking four more cruises contingent on their satisfaction with this one. I really want it to go well."

Russ was silent so long, Carly turned to look at him. "What's wrong?"

"You didn't ask whatsisname about becoming a silent partner yet, did you?"

"No. I wanted to think about it a little longer. Why?"

"Because I've got a little surprise that I think will make you happy. When I suggested you look into getting a silent partner, I was hoping you'd think of me."

Carly blinked. "You?"

"Sure. It's the perfect setup, especially since we'll be married."

Carly felt uneasiness crawl under her skin. "Well, we can think about that later. We've got enough to do now."

Russ lifted a broad shoulder in a half-shrug. "It's already a done deal. I bought your brothers' share of *Matilda's Dream* about a month ago."

The world tilted. Stunned, Carly shook her head to clear it. She couldn't have heard correctly. "You're not saying you've already bought it?"

Russ nodded. "They've been paid."

Something heavy settled in her chest. It made it hard for her to breathe. "But they didn't tell me," she said, confused. "You didn't tell me."

Russ cleared his throat and quickly glanced at her. "Well, I kinda asked them not to discuss it. I thought it would be better if you and I worked out our, uh, personal relationship first."

"You didn't think to discuss this with me?" Her voice shook from the turmoil inside her. This sounded as though it was all part of a plan to keep her under control. She felt an ominous sense of betrayal. All her brothers and Russ had planned this without consulting her. The professional doubter on her shoulder reminded her that Russ still hadn't said he loved her.

"Carly," he began in that placating tone that made her grind her teeth, "I thought it was for the best and—"

Her hurt and confusion exploded into fiery anger. "*You* thought it was best! What about what I thought? What if I don't want you to be my partner? What if I think it's a horrible idea?"

"How could it be horrible? We're going to be partners in marriage. Why not in business? This way, you won't have to worry about your brothers interfering."

"No. I'll just have to worry about you interfering." She was so hurt and furious, she was ready to pop a blood vessel. She had to get away from him. "Stop the car and pull over."

"Carly—"

"Don't you Carly me. Pull over or I swear I won't wait until you stop to get out of this car."

His jaw tightened, and he pulled the car onto the curb. "You're not being rational."

"Rational! Why should I worry about being rational? You're rational enough for everybody." Carly unclipped her seat belt and shoved open her car door.

Russ checked his rearview mirror for oncoming

traffic and followed her out of the car. "I didn't think you'd get upset. I thought you'd be grateful."

"Grateful!" she yelled. "Grateful because you and my brothers are manipulating me and my business. L-L-Leave m-me-" She cursed at the untimely stutter and waved her arm in frustration. "Y-You know what I mean. Leave me alone!"

Russ stared after her as she stalked down the road, digging her high heels into the gravel and dirt. "I can't let you walk all the way into town. Be reasonable." When she didn't respond, Russ exhaled in exasperation and took off after her. It only took a few swift strides before he caught up with her and touched her on the shoulder.

She spun around with tears on her face and fury in her eyes. "I trusted you. I loved you, dammit. And then you went behind my back." She backed away. "Get away. I never want to see you again."

It was the first time she'd said she loved him out loud, and it did something to his guts. Russ stretched out his arms, reaching for her. "Carly, we can work—"

She pulled off one of her shoes, and Russ watched in disbelief as she threw it at him. She barely missed her target, which Russ grimly suspected was his crotch. Horrified, he ducked when she tossed the other one. Then she turned and ran down the road on her bare feet.

Russ hurried back to the truck and followed her even after she hitched a ride with Mr. Perkins, the old man who ran the vegetable stand. She didn't waste a single glance on her new fiancé, Russ noticed. He gnawed the inside of his cheek as he watched her go into her apartment. She hadn't said a word about their engagement, but Russ had the sinking feeling that this was one mess up he might not be able to fix. It left a hollow, lonely feeling inside him, worse than he'd ever felt before.

Surprisingly, the cruise went off without a hitch. Carly gritted her teeth and smiled graciously when she really wanted to spit nails. After she returned to her apartment, she was still too angry to sleep. Adrenaline rushed through her veins like caffeine. She spent the whole night flailing herself for her foolishness. She should have caught on to Russ Bradford and his tricks. The slime.

And her brothers. She hoped the Ladies Auxiliary descended on them like a horde of bees. It was the least they deserved.

She didn't know whether she was more angry or hurt at Russ's lie of omission. But she clung to the anger, because hurting and pining over a man who hadn't ever said he loved her seemed the height of stupidity.

By the following afternoon, Sara had taken several messages from her brothers. "Daniel wants to know when you'll return his call," Sara said.

"After Christmas, if I'm feeling generous," Carly said.

Sara gave a little smile. "I'll tell him."

Carly noticed the satisfaction on Sara's face. "You look like you'll enjoy it too. You never told me what happened that day you helped Daniel."

Sara nodded, her mouth tightening grimly. "He's a member of your family, so I didn't want to insult you."

Carly laughed for the first time that day. "Insult me. I need a good laugh."

Propriety warred with feminine pique on Sara's face. Feminine pique won. "He was incredibly rude," she burst out. "First he was angry that I had shown up to help him instead of you. Then, he wouldn't let me feed him the soup." She rolled her eyes. "I've never met a more independent man. When I finally coaxed him into letting me feed him, he started lecturing me about what a bad influence I've been over you. Between," Sara announced incredulously, "the barhopping and the mail-order lingerie."

Carly choked on her amused gasp. "You didn't let him get away with it, did you?"

Sara looked suddenly uncomfortable. "Well, no."

"What did you do?"

"I tried to give him the rest of the soup, but he didn't want any help. He started waving his arms, and it ended up in his lap."

Carly howled. "Oh, I wish I'd been there. What did he do?"

"He yelled and I left. When he called just now, he pretended it never happened."

"Yeah. Male pride." Carly sobered, thinking of Russ, wondering if he'd be able to pretend their relationship had never happened. "Speaking of male pride, I have a new business partner. My backbone-less brothers sold out to Russ."

Sara widened her eyes. "Russ? Hmmm. Sounds like their clumsy way of making sure you're taken care of."

"In more ways than one. I think they wanted me to marry him too."

"Well, it's obvious that's what Russ wants," Sara observed. "He hasn't hidden his feelings about you—calling everyday, stopping by to check on you, sending flowers. And now he's bought out your brothers. It sounds like a perfect solution to your owning the riverboat outright."

Carly blinked. "It does?"

"Sure. Now you get to be the boss without financially strapping yourself."

"I hadn't really thought of it that way," Carly admitted quietly.

"Why not?"

Carly felt her skin prickle with heat. "The timing was off. I'd just told him I would marry him."

"You're getting married?" Sara's voice raised a notch.

Carly winced. "Well, no. I think it's safe to say the engagement's off. After I threw my shoes at him, he left me alone." Carly couldn't endure Sara's look of censure. "They did it behind my back," she said hotly. "Didn't bother to consult me." She waved her arm. "Just arranged my life as if I were an idiot."

Sara frowned, shaking her head. "It's hard to believe Russ did that."

"He said it was a *surprise*. He thought I'd be grateful." With the first blinding rush of her anger blunted, Carly wondered if she and Russ had misunderstood each other. Talking it out with Sara made her feel confused.

"Did he try to explain?"

"Yes," Carly admitted, "but I just felt too manipulated to listen. It was like he poked my one sore spot." Why did all of this sound so lame today?

Sara's eyes were filled with concern. "If you don't trust him and if you really believe he's that much of a manipulator, then I guess it's a good thing you're not going to marry him."

"I didn't say I don't trust—" The phone rang, and she stopped.

"I'll get that," Sara said, exiting the room.

Carly stared after her. Sara was only repeating Carly. So why did she feel this sudden need to defend Russ? Why did she feel compelled to clarify and explain?

They should have consulted her, part of her insisted. To hear Sara tell it, though, Russ was giving her what she wanted—like any man who wanted to impress the woman he planned to marry. It had been an expensive, almost flamboyant gesture for such a prudent, practical man to make, she thought. Anybody else might call it a gesture of love. Carly's stomach sank.

Had she been so busy watching for the words that she'd been blind to his actions? People say it all the time and it doesn't mean a thing, he'd said. People make promises they don't keep. Gwen hadn't kept hers to Russ, and Carly had already taken back hers. Her angry words left a bitter taste in her mouth.

Carly bit her lip against a wave of regret. Lord, what a mess she'd made. She bowed her head and covered her face with her hands. It all looked different now. Russ had busted a gut to win her over. He'd put himself on the line repeatedly. Like the night on the boat when he'd given to her so generously. He'd been tender and caring, sensing the healing she'd needed. He'd freed something inside her that night. She hadn't recognized it until now, but Carly had let go of grief that had kept her bound until that night. He'd taken a deep hurt and ministered to it, showing her life could be different for her now.

The image of his face, lined with crushing disappointment, haunted her, stabbing her conscience. She'd hurt him badly, she realized. There was no one to blame but herself, and the heavy weight of remorse settled over her like a cloak. She'd hurt the one person who'd shown her more love than anyone else in her entire life. Carly squeezed her eyes shut, but the shame scraped her heart, leaving her raw.

She deserved it, Carly thought. She deserved every stab of shame, every bit of stomach turning self-disgust. But the realization that nearly shocked her with a doubling over kind of pain was that she did not deserve Russ.

With his fierce male pride, the only thing that would have made it worse was if she'd spurned him in public. Carly took small comfort in the fact that no one had witnessed her tirade.

Sunday morning dawned gray and rainy. The weather mirrored her spirit, and Carly was tempted to skip church. She felt miserable and confused. But she knew if she stayed away, she'd have to deal with twice as much flack.

She shrugged on her most boring navy dress and prayed no one would give her a second glance. She crept into an empty pew near the back and spent most of the service trying not to look for Russ.

Halfway through the sermon, she spotted him. His face was set in somber lines. He wore a navy suit that didn't look the least bit boring on his broad shoulders and muscular frame. He narrowed his eyes and turned slightly. Her stomach somersaulted when he almost looked at her.

By the time the pastor gave the benediction, her palms were sweating. Just two days ago she'd begged him to leave her alone. Today she wasn't sure what she wanted, but she knew the distance between them was more than seven pews. The dreadful loss she felt made her sick.

She managed to scoot out the back and made it to the steps where she paused to raise her umbrella. "Excuse me," she murmured, feeling someone at her back.

Then she looked up and there he was, rain in his hair and bitter surprise in his eyes. She braced herself for his angry words. She deserved them.

"Hey, Russ," one of his friends called. "Hear you're dodging spiked heels. Better get yourself some armor." Then the guy hooted with laughter and nudged the man beside him.

Carly nearly lost her breakfast. They all knew. She clenched her fists, wishing there was something she could do to rectify the situation. She looked at Russ and thought he was finally going to speak to her, probably curse her to hell. But didn't. He looked right through her as if she weren't there, and walked away. He did exactly what she'd asked him to do, she realized. He left her alone.

Word must have spread fast, because Troy and Daniel confronted her that afternoon at her apartment while she folded laundry.

"Why won't you marry him?" Troy asked.

Daniel shook his head. "I still can't believe you threw your shoes at him."

She couldn't either. "I don't have a good explanation. All I can tell you is that things are complicated. It didn't help that you sold your part of *Matilda's Dream* without discussing it with me."

Daniel shifted. "That was Russ's idea."

Troy's expression was pure censure. "He wanted to surprise you."

"I was definitely surprised."

"So, what are you gonna do now?"

Carly sighed, fighting an overwhelming urge to sob.

Since she'd seen Russ at church, she'd been teetering on the edge of an emotional cliff. "I, uh." Her voice shook and she swallowed hard, taking an inordinately long time to fold a T-shirt. "I'm not sure."

She watched her brothers exchange a look of discomfort. They could handle anything but her tears. She hoped she'd be able to spare them.

"Listen, Carly," Troy said, "if Bradford's done any-thing to uh—" He shrugged. "Anything to, you know—" He flicked out his hand impatiently. "You know what I mean, Daniel. You tell her."

"Hey, don't look at me."

Troy frowned. "If Bradford's done anything to com-promise you, let us know and we'll take care of it."

If she'd been in another mood, she would have laughed. Instead, she knew she'd have to word her response carefully or the relationship between Russ and her brothers would fracture, and Carly didn't want that. "Russ hasn't done anything for you to worry about."

Troy let out a long relieved breath and nodded. "Okay. Well, we better be going."

They walked toward the door, and Carly gave Troy, then Daniel a hug.

"Are you gonna try to talk to him?" Daniel asked in a low voice.

"It might be a little late for that."

He raised his eyebrows. "Better late than never, little sister." Then they left, and Carly closed the door behind them.

After five more lonely, tear-filled nights, Carly learned something important about herself. She learned Russ had become the light in her darkest night and nobody else would take his place. That fact gave her the courage to lay it on the line and tell Russ how wrong she'd been.

Friday afternoon, she put out feelers for locating him, but nobody knew where he was. Ethan, Nathan, and Brick had just arrived back from their camping trip. When Carly quizzed them about where the rest of her brothers were, they mentioned Western Willie's bar. It clicked in her mind. How appropriate, she thought, and headed for her closet.

Taking a deep breath, she pulled out her armor and got ready for peace talks.

Eleven

This was a mistake, Russ decided after drinking half a beer. He glanced around the noisy bar and brooded. He wasn't fit to face the rest of humanity. He was miserable, and he preferred keeping his misery to himself. Instead he was surrounded by a Friday night crowd determined to shake off the workweek. Men and women alternately gyrated and clung to one another as songs about whiskey and women played around them.

"You ready for another one?" Garth asked when the waitress checked on them.

He shook his head. "Nah. I think I'll be heading out when I finish this one. It's been a long day."

"You can't do that," Jarod said. "We just got here. Ethan, Nathan, and Brick might be coming by." He nudged Troy with his elbow.

Troy gave Jarod a brief glare, then turned a friendly grimace toward Russ. "That's right. Let me get you some peanuts and you'll be ready for that next beer in no time."

Russ gave a noncommittal nod. It was unsettling for Troy to act so nice. Seeing four grown men tiptoe around the reason for his sour mood made him feel even more testy. He'd rather hit somebody than drink beer tonight. But Carly's brothers weren't giving him the opportunity. They hadn't mentioned her name once. And they were being so nice, it made him feel as though he were wearing brand-new shoes—damned uncomfortable.

"How'd that last harvest turn out?" Daniel asked. "I worried about you having enough time for your own work with all you did for me."

"Don't give it a second thought. I did fine. It's nice to know I'll be able to count on you if I get hit by a disaster." As soon as he said it, Russ realized he'd already been hit by disaster. She was five feet ten with big violet eyes and a crimson mouth that had the ability to render him mindless. She was also the woman who'd stolen his heart, lock, stock, and barrel. Frowning, Russ raised his mug and finished it in three swallows.

"There you go," Troy said with excess cheer as he passed a bowl to Russ. "Nothing like pretzels and—" He broke off, finishing with a barnyard curse.

Jarod looked at Troy, then into the crowd. His face fell. "What is she doing here?"

Garth scowled.

"I thought I told ya'll not to tell her where we were going tonight," Daniel said in a threatening tone.

Feeling a tingling premonition, Russ searched the crowd and saw her, teetering on mile-high heels, wearing that man-eater dress, and impatiently shaking off an admirer's searching hands. Russ's stomach twisted into a knot.

Brick came up behind her and put a heavy hand

on the guy's shoulder. Ethan and Nathan backed up Brick with menacing glances while Carly's determined gaze found Russ. Then she left the lot of them in her wake.

Russ looked down at his empty mug. Where was a double shot of whiskey when you needed it?

At the same time the waitress replaced his beer, Carly came to a halt beside his chair. The waitress wasn't the bashful kind. She set a napkin with a phone number on the table and winked. "I get off at midnight."

His gaze slid to Carly, and he watched while the wind seemed to go out of her sails. Her violet eyes lost their spark, and she suddenly looked unsure.

No more unsure than he was, he thought and slouched in his chair. "I'll remember that," he murmured to the waitress.

He felt Carly stiffen beside him. She crossed her arms over her chest. Russ caught a whiff of her sultry scent and stifled a groan. "Hi, Carly," he managed in his most casual tone.

"Hi. I, uh, wanted to tell you something." She looked around as if she were having second thoughts.

He shrugged. "Go ahead." From the corner of his eye, he noticed all her brothers were staring at her.

Carly shifted. Her shiny earrings jiggled below her ears, catching the light. She swatted at the distraction. Russ remembered kissing her there where she was particularly sensitive. She'd laughed breathlessly. He clamped his jaw together. This casual slouch was getting a little tough to maintain.

She shifted her shoulders. The sleeve fell a little farther down her arm. Russ thought she was looking at his ear. She sure as hell wasn't looking at his eyes.

"It probably won't make any difference to you, but I wanted you to know." She cleared her throat. "I was wrong the other day. I acted horrible, and—" She took a deep breath and looked at the ceiling. "You probably won't be able to forgive me, but I'm really—"

He watched her swallow and felt his chest ache when he saw the moist sheen in her eyes. She finally met his gaze.

"I'm sorry, Russ. I'm r-r-really sorry."

Russ stared at her. A public apology. She could have knocked him over with her pinkie finger.

After a moment, she broke the gaze and started to turn away. Russ's reflexes returned like lightning. He reached out and snared her wrist. "Is that all?" he asked roughly over his dry throat.

Her eyebrows furrowed in confusion. "All?"

"Is that all you wanted to tell me?"

"Oh," she murmured, her features clearing. She shook her wrist within his grip. He tightened his hand, then deliberately loosened it. Her hand slipped away, but she surprised him by lacing her fingers with his. "I wanted to tell you that I love you," she said in a crystal clear voice.

His heart pounded hard against his rib cage.

"You're the most important man in my life." Her eyes darkened with emotion. "There's a lot of things I've never done before, and I'd like to do them all with you."

Russ heard Troy mutter something in the background. Russ stood, ignoring curious stares. Still wary, he warned, "I can't take this hot and cold stuff anymore."

"Then I'll make it easy. Will you marry me?"

The building could have fallen down around him,

and he wouldn't have known it. His insides turned to mush at the love in her eyes. He brought her hand to his chest so she could feel how she affected him. His heart was racing a mile a minute. Her lips curved into a slow, tentative smile.

He smiled back, knowing he probably looked like a grinning fool. "Yes, I'll marry you. But, Carly, if you wear that dress in public again, you'll have to bail your husband out of jail."

"Why?"

"'Cause I'll kill anybody who looks at you."

She laughed. "Guess I'd better take it off."

Russ shook his head, distantly heard Brick's exclamation of disapproval, then curved his hand around her neck, drawing her closer to kiss her. Her lips parted sweetly, and Russ felt as though he were coming home to warmth and love. After a moment of tasting her, he rested his forehead against hers. "Let's get out of here."

She drew a shaky breath. "Fine with me."

Russ picked her up in his arms.

"Hey, Bradford," Troy said, "you're not officially married yet."

"That's okay," Russ said over his shoulder. "She can't renege. You heard her. I've got witnesses this time."

"I wasn't worried about Carly backing out," Troy griped.

"Aw, can it, Troy," Daniel said.

"You sure have been a grouch lately. What's your problem?" The squabbling faded as Russ carried Carly from the bar. He shook his head again, this time in disbelief. His commitment had never been in question.

Russ looked down at Carly. "You know you stunned me."

She gave a wry smile. "So I have a little bit of an effect on you?"

"About like a heart attack."

"Oh, your heart. Sounds serious."

He came to a stop. "You know I love you."

Carly nodded. "Yeah." Then she reached up and kissed him, and all the kidding left her expression. "But it sure feels good to hear it."

His chest swelled, remembering how it had felt for her to announce her love in front of that crowd of people. He vowed to do the same for her. He didn't want any doubts between them ever again. "I love you." He held her tighter, cherishing the weight of her precious feminine body. "I won't let you forget it."

Epilogue

"Hey, Carly," Brick called through the door to her cabin on *Matilda's Dream*. He gave a few raps, then burst in. "Everybody's waiting. You need to get the lead—" He stopped and stared. "You look like a fairy princess. Where'd you get the dress?"

Carly took the boutonniere and pin from his hand and attached it to the lapel of his tuxedo. "Chattanooga. Is Russ here?"

Brick shrugged. "I don't know. Maybe he wised up and headed for the hills."

"Brick, I've got a sharp pin in my hand," she warned her biggest brother. He had a sense of humor about everything but his given name. That's why anyone who wanted to keep their teeth called him Brick.

"You stab me and I'll turn you over my knee."

She lifted her chin. "I've got somebody just as big as you to stand up for me now."

He gave a wry grin. "Guess you do at that." Then

he turned serious. "He's a good man, Carly. You couldn't do better."

Her eyes misted, and she blinked. Her emotions had been tugging at her all day. "I know. I just hope all of you find someone who'll love you like this one day." She wrapped her arms around him and a sob escaped.

"Hey," he chided her, holding her. "You're supposed to be all smiles. None of this crying stuff."

"I know. I'm just happy."

He patted her on the back. "Well, if this is happy, think about something depressing. Maybe it'll balance out."

Carly laughed through her tears and pushed him toward the door. "Okay, go on out. Let me fix my makeup one last time."

Brick paused. "Mom would be proud."

Carly touched her mother's pearl necklace at her throat and nodded, feeling another spate of tears threaten. When he left, she fanned her face and dabbed at her tears with a tissue.

Sara stepped in, seeming to float in pale blue chiffon. Smiling in gentle understanding, she arranged the lace-trimmed veil that trailed down Carly's back from a wreath around her crown. "You really do look beautiful. This dress is perfect for you."

"Think so?" Carly smoothed the Queen Anne neckline, touching the beads and iridescent sequins that embellished the richly detailed bodice and pouf sleeves. Embroidered cutouts and scalloped lace accented the satin train. Carly lifted the hem, revealing white satin ballet slippers. "I couldn't risk heels today. I'm too shaky."

"You'll be fine. Here's a lace handkerchief for something borrowed." Sara pressed the fine fabric in her hand. "The pearls are something old. And your ring is something blue and new."

Carly looked at the one-carat diamond set off by twin sapphire baguettes on either side. It flashed and sparkled every time she moved her hand. "It's hard for me to believe it's mine." She took a deep breath. "It's hard to believe that Russ is mine."

There was another knock on the door. "It's time," Sara said. "Are you ready?" She kissed Carly on the cheek and handed her the bouquet of long-stemmed American Beauty roses.

Carly nodded and they left the room where Daniel waited for her. Sara and Daniel made an extraordinary effort not to notice each other, but it looked as though both were failing. Carly smiled, and a few steps later, she was walking out onto the deck lit with a hundred lights under a clear starry sky. A trio of strings played Wagner.

Carly looked across the crowd of people. It seemed as though the whole town was here, the mayor and his family, church members. She winked at her brothers.

Then she saw Russ. He shared the front with Garth and the minister, but he shared his gaze only with Carly. The wind played with his red hair. The white shirt was a sharp contrast with his tanned skin and his black tuxedo.

He stared at her, seemingly entranced. Then he smiled and her heart was full, so full. He took her hand when she reached him. He felt warm and solid.

"Who gives this woman?" the minister asked in his booming voice.

All seven of her brothers stood. "We do," they said in unison.

Then Carly faced Russ, absorbing his confidence

and love, and traded vows. Miraculously, she managed not to stutter. But she sensed it wouldn't have mattered to Russ even if she had. He loved her just the way she was.

Everything turned into a blur after Russ pushed the gold band on her finger. The minister said something about kissing the bride. Russ grinned broadly and wrapped her in a fierce embrace. Then he kissed her. Another promise. She felt it in his lips, in his arms.

Carly couldn't hold back the tears any longer. They streamed freely down her cheeks.

With a not-so-steady hand, he brushed the moisture from her skin. "You'll never know how happy you've made me, Carly."

To her surprise, she saw a telltale shimmer of liquid in his brown eyes. "Oh, Russ."

"There's something I want you to see. Look over there." He turned her chin toward an archway of tiny white lights at the other end of the boat.

Carly gasped, then hiccuped over the lump in her throat. The lights were arranged to spell out the words "Russ loves Carly." "Everyone will know now."

His eyes were serious. "I just need for you to know."

Her heart nearly burst. She was living a dream come true. "Oh, I do," she assured him, and made plans to assure him every day of her life.

And later that night, Russ showed Carly his new tattoo.

THE EDITOR'S CORNER

What could be more romantic than Valentine's Day and six LOVESWEPT romances all in one glorious month! Celebrate this special time of the year by cuddling up with the wonderful books coming your way soon.

The first of our reading treasures is **ANGELS SINGING** by Joan Elliott Pickart, LOVESWEPT #594. Drew Sloan's first impression of Memory Lawson isn't the best, considering she's pointing a shotgun at him and accusing him of trespassing on her mountain. But the heat that flashes between them convinces him to stay and storm the walls around her heart . . . until she believes that she's just the kind of warm, loving woman he's been looking for. Joan comes through once more with a winning romance!

We have a real treat in store for fans of Kay Hooper. After a short hiatus for work on **THE DELANEY CHRISTMAS CAROL** and other books, Kay returns with **THE TOUCH OF MAX,** LOVESWEPT #595, the *fiftieth* book in her illustrious career! If you were a fan of Kay's popular "Hagan Strikes Again" and "Once Upon a Time" series, you'll be happy to know that **THE TOUCH OF MAX** is the first of four "Men of Mysteries Past" books, all of which center around Max Bannister's priceless gem collection, which the police are using as bait to catch a notorious thief. But when innocent Dinah Layton gets tangled in the trap, it'll take that special touch of Max to set her free . . . and capture her heart. A sheer delight—and it'll have you breathlessly waiting for more. Welcome back, Kay!

In Charlotte Hughes's latest novel, Crescent City's new soccer coach is **THE INCREDIBLE HUNK,** LOVE-SWEPT #596. Utterly male, gorgeously virile, Jason Profitt has the magic touch with kids. What more perfect guy could there be for a redhead with five children to raise! But Maggie Farnsworth is sure that once he's seen her chaotic life, he'll run for the hills. Jason has another plan of action in mind, though—to make a home in her loving arms. Charlotte skillfully blends humor and passion in this page-turner of a book.

Appropriately enough, Marcia Evanick's contribution to the month, **OVER THE RAINBOW,** LOVESWEPT #597, is set in a small town called Oz, where neither Hillary Walker nor Mitch Ferguson suspects his kids of matchmaking when he's forced to meet the lovely speech teacher. The plan works so well the kids are sure they'll get a mom for Christmas. But Hillary has learned never to trust her heart again, and only Mitch's passionate persuasion can change her mind. You can count on Marcia to deliver a fun-filled romance.

A globetrotter in buckskins and a beard, Nick Leclerc has never considered himself **THE FOREVER MAN,** LOVESWEPT #598, by Joan J. Domning. Yet when he appears in Carla Hudson's salon for a haircut and a shave, her touch sets his body on fire and fills him with unquenchable longing. The sexy filmmaker has leased Carla's ranch to uncover an ancient secret, but instead he finds newly awakened dreams of hearth and home. Joan will capture your heart with this wonderful love story.

Erica Spindler finishes this dazzling month with **TEMPT-ING CHANCE,** LOVESWEPT #599. Shy Beth Waters doesn't think she has what it takes to light the sensual spark in gorgeous Chance Michaels. But the outrageous results of her throwing away a chain letter finally convince her that she's woman enough to tempt Chance— and that he's more than eager to be caught in her embrace. Humorous, yet seething with emotion and desire, **TEMPTING CHANCE** is one tempting morsel from talented Erica.

Look for four spectacular novels on sale now from FANFARE. Award-winning Iris Johansen confirms her place as a major star with **THE TIGER PRINCE,** a magnificent new historical romance that sweeps from exotic realms to the Scottish highlands. In a locked room of shadows and sandalwood, Jane Barnaby meets adventurer Ruel McClaren and is instantly transformed from a hard-headed businesswoman to the slave of a passion she knows she must resist.

Suzanne Robinson first introduced us to Blade in **LADY GALLANT,** and now in the new thrilling historical romance **LADY DEFIANT,** Blade returns as a bold, dashing hero. One of Queen Elizabeth's most dangerous spies, he must romance a beauty named Oriel who holds a clue that could change history. Desire builds and sparks fly as these two unwillingly join forces to thwart a deadly conspiracy.

Hailed by Katherine Stone as "emotional, compelling, and triumphant!", **PRIVATE SCANDALS** is the debut novel by very talented Christy Cohen. From the glamour of New York to the glitter of Hollywood comes a heartfelt story of scandalous desires and long-held secrets . . . of dreams realized and longings denied . . . of three remarkable women whose lifelong friendship would be threatened by one man.

Available once again is **A LOVE FOR ALL TIME** by bestselling author Dorothy Garlock. In this moving tale, Casey Farrow gives up all hope of a normal life when a car crash leaves indelible marks on her breathtaking beauty . . . until Dan Farrow, the man who rescued her from the burning vehicle, convinces her that he loves her just the way she is.

Also on sale this month in the hardcover edition from Doubleday is **THE LADY AND THE CHAMP** by Fran Baker. When a former Golden Gloves champion meets an elegant, uptown girl, the result is a stirring novel of courageous love that Julie Garwood has hailed as "unforgettable."

Happy reading!

With warmest wishes,

Nita Taublib

Nita Taublib
Associate Publisher
LOVESWEPT and FANFARE

OFFICIAL RULES TO WINNERS CLASSIC SWEEPSTAKES

No Purchase necessary. To enter the sweepstakes follow instructions found elsewhere in this offer. You can also enter the sweepstakes by hand printing your name, address, city, state and zip code on a 3" x 5" piece of paper and mailing it to: Winners Classic Sweepstakes, P.O. Box 785, Gibbstown, NJ 08027. Mail each entry separately. Sweepstakes begins 12/1/91. Entries must be received by 6/1/93. Some presentations of this sweepstakes may feature a deadline for the Early Bird prize. If the offer you receive does, then to be eligible for the Early Bird prize your entry must be received according to the Early Bird date specified. Not responsible for lost, late, damaged, misdirected, illegible or postage due mail. Mechanically reproduced entries are not eligible. All entries become property of the sponsor and will not be returned.

Prize Selection/Validations: Winners will be selected in random drawings on or about 7/30/93, by VENTURA ASSOCIATES, INC., an independent judging organization whose decisions are final. Odds of winning are determined by total number of entries received. Circulation of this sweepstakes is estimated not to exceed 200 million. Entrants need not be present to win. All prizes are guaranteed to be awarded and delivered to winners. Winners will be notified by mail and may be required to complete an affidavit of eligibility and release of liability which must be returned within 14 days of date of notification or alternate winners will be selected. Any guest of a trip winner will also be required to execute a release of liability. Any prize notification letter or any prize returned to a participating sponsor, Bantam Doubleday Dell Publishing Group, Inc., its participating divisions or subsidiaries, or VENTURA ASSOCIATES, INC. as undeliverable will be awarded to an alternate winner. Prizes are not transferable. No multiple prize winners except as may be necessary due to unavailability, in which case a prize of equal or greater value will be awarded. Prizes will be awarded approximately 90 days after the drawing. All taxes, automobile license and registration fees, if applicable, are the sole responsibility of the winners. Entry constitutes permission (except where prohibited) to use winners' names and likenesses for publicity purposes without further or other compensation.

Participation: This sweepstakes is open to residents of the United States and Canada, except for the province of Quebec. This sweepstakes is sponsored by Bantam Doubleday Dell Publishing Group, Inc. (BDD), 666 Fifth Avenue, New York, NY 10103. Versions of this sweepstakes with different graphics will be offered in conjunction with various solicitations or promotions by different subsidiaries and divisions of BDD. Employees and their families of BDD, its division, subsidiaries, advertising agencies, and VENTURA ASSOCIATES, INC., are not eligible.

Canadian residents, in order to win, must first correctly answer a time limited arithmetical skill testing question. Void in Quebec and wherever prohibited or restricted by law. Subject to all federal, state, local and provincial laws and regulations.

Prizes: The following values for prizes are determined by the manufacturers' suggested retail prices or by what these items are currently known to be selling for at the time this offer was published. Approximate retail values include handling and delivery of prizes. Estimated maximum retail value of prizes: 1 Grand Prize ($27,500 if merchandise or $25,000 Cash); 1 First Prize ($3,000); 5 Second Prizes ($400 each); 35 Third Prizes ($100 each); 1,000 Fourth Prizes ($9.00 each) ; 1 Early Bird Prize ($5,000); Total approximate maximum retail value is $50,000. Winners will have the option of selecting any prize offered at level won. Automobile winner must have a valid driver's license at the time the car is awarded. Trips are subject to space and departure availability. Certain black-out dates may apply. Travel must be completed within one year from the time the prize is awarded. Minors must be accompanied by an adult. Prizes won by minors will be awarded in the name of parent or legal guardian.

For a list of Major Prize Winners (available after 7/30/93): send a self-addressed, stamped envelope entirely separate from your entry to: Winners Classic Sweepstakes Winners, P.O. Box 825, Gibbstown, NJ 08027. Requests must be received by 6/1/93. DO NOT SEND ANY OTHER CORRESPONDENCE TO THIS P.O. BOX.